A Time for Heroes

Dorman,

By D. Bruce Coryell

Bruce Coryell

Published by D. Bruce Coryell

Martindale, Texas

ISBN 978-1-61422-905-6

Printed in the U.S. by Instantpublisher.com

Acknowledgements

My thanks to Tipton and Ann Golias for their superior editing and support for my writing.

In recognition of Gerardo Baranovicht for sharing his story with me, and thus planting the seeds that resulted in this novel.

My deepest gratitude to my wife, Chris, who worked tirelessly to improve the story line and make sure what I said made sense...really made sense.

Heartfelt thanks to Jerry Waller for the invaluable information he provided regarding the military, and for his selfless service to our country.

Many thanks to my daughter, Kara, who provided hours of research to this project.

Lastly, my thanks to all the many people who have enriched my life and whose personalities and character I borrowed from in the writing of this novel.

"INSCRIPTION ON THE STATUE OF LIBERTY"

Give me your tired, your poor,

Your huddled masses, yearning to breathe free,

The wretched refuse of your teeming shore,

Send these, the homeless, tempest tossed to me,

I lift my lamp beside the golden door.

Author: Emma Lazarus

CHAPTER I

My name is Gerardo Moises Baranovicht. My Chinese grandfather on my mother's side, Jose Esteban Lau, was born in 1900 in Canton, China. My other grandfather, Emigdio Enrique Baranovicht, was born in Belarus. My story, and that of my family, begins with them. In many ways it is also the story of the thousands of other desperate families from Central America who shared the dream of coming to the United States to escape from the ravages of war, poverty, and persecution.

China   Early March, 1927

Jose Esteban Lau stood silently by the portside rail of the *Empress of Canada*. Behind him on the ship's starboard side and hidden from his view, a flotilla of tugboats working at full throttle, pulled her away from the dock in an attempt to get her bow pointed in the direction that would take her out of Hong Kong's harbor and into the South China Sea. It was the beginning of a voyage which would take him across the vastness of the Pacific Ocean, first to Hawaii, and then San Francisco. From there he would take a coastal steamer southward along the coast of Mexico to his adopted country of Nicaragua.

With him on the deck were hundreds of other Chinese men, women, and children, crowding the rail in order to wave goodbye to their families. For many of them it would be their final contact with their family and loved ones. Well educated in the history of his people, Jose knew they were part of an exodus of the Chinese people brought to the United States to work for the railroad companies. That earlier exodus began in the middle of the last century and was continuing still, but no longer at the urging of the railroads. Now, they came for jobs, any job that would free them from the grinding poverty they had been born to.

As they pressed against him, Jose began to look for his family, while at the same time painfully aware it was a pointless search. His own family, at his request, was not among the throngs of people on the dock.

"Because of my love for each of you," he had told them in a hushed voice on the verge of failing him, "if any of you are on the dock to see me off, I'm not sure I will have the strength to go aboard."

As one, but with a visible reluctance, his family agreed to honor his request.

Now, as the dark watery opening between the ship and the dock grew larger with each passing second, he realized he had only considered his own feelings, and not the hurt his request would cause them...the same chest tightening hurt he was now experiencing.

"I was a dammed fool to throw away my last chance to see them," he told himself.

A series of ear bursting blasts from the ship's horn shocked his thoughts out of the present and back to the past, back to the family meeting which had taken place four days earlier in his mother's bedroom.

After quietly entering their mother's bedroom, Jose, his three brothers and one sister, had reverently bowed their heads in their mother's direction before moving to the side of her bed and placing soft kisses on her lightly powdered cheeks. With that formality concluded, they seated themselves on the cushioned chairs placed on the window side of the large four-poster bed. Years before, the bed had belonged to a high ranking English official, but to his misfortune, his gambling losses invariably exceeded the size of his pocketbook. As a result, the bed, made in London from aged English oak, was now his mother's most prized piece of furniture…and on it her last two children had been conceived and born.

Years later, she became bedridden because of a crippling condition shared by thousands of other women. Like the others, while still an infant, her parents, in order to make her feet 'tiny and beautiful' in accordance with an ancient belief, had bound her feet in a way which curled her toes forward and severely deformed the arches of her feet. This painful deformity forced her toes to curl under and inward. From early childhood, she had to take short, choppy steps when walking, and as an adult, she could barely walk without some form of assistance.

The bed, which was often referred to by her children as 'the throne,' now rested on a foot high pedestal from which she conducted business and guided her family's fortune.

As the years passed and she became a wife and then a mother, what she lacked in mobility, she made up for with an iron will and a never ending dogged determination to secure all that was possible for her family. Even before her husband's death, Ling Lee's was a stern but loving dictatorship over her family… and an intimidating presence among the business world of Canton.

Jose knew it was not a coincidence that he and his brothers and sister were seated on chairs which kept their heads slightly below that of their mother. He also knew the elevated bed gave her a slight psychological advantage over her visitors. His mother's visitors, when summoned to her bedside, accepted her position above them out of respect and as a necessary business practice. Her children accepted her action out of both affection and respect for her authority, but just as importantly, to honor her as their mother.

3

He also realized the presence of his mother's treasured porcelain tea setting, made in the city of Longquan and given to her as a wedding gift, was an unspoken signal to her children that this was to be a meeting of a serious nature.

Because he was the first of her children to enter the room, Ling Lee took the opportunity it offered to once again admire the appearance of her eldest son, the son whom she named Chi Chu at birth. Although now using the ugly sounding name given to him by her brother Patricio, to her joy, he was the same beautiful son she had sent to that far away country as a twelve year old boy. Only months ago, he returned home as a very impressive looking twenty-eight year old man. To her, it was a notable transformation.

Unlike his brothers who resembled her side of the family in both size and facial features, Chi Chu had inherited the musculature and height of her husband's family. He was slender, but not thin, with pronounced muscles which were evident, even under the loosest of garments. At nearly six feet tall he was several inches above the height of what was considered to be tall for the average a Chinese male.

"If he had a long lovely queue hanging to the small of his back, instead of keeping his hair cut so short," she thought wistfully, "he would be the reincarnation of my dear husband."

All of these things she found great pleasure in, but what she found most pleasing, the thing which made her long for the early days of marriage, was how closely his facial features resembled those of his father. He had the same eyes as his father, eyes which could change in an instant from puppy soft to those of a menacing wolf.

Also, like his father's eyes, Chi Chu's eyes seemed to have an exceptional intelligence and playfulness behind them. It was this last feature which

4

she liked to think of as a solid clue that 'just perhaps he is not entirely his father's son.'

From the day he arrived back in Canton after a thirteen year absence, Jose had been amazed at how little his mother's appearance had changed from what he remembered from his childhood. To his eyes she was still as beautiful as ever. It was as if she was impervious to the passing of time. He hadn't failed to notice a touch of gray in her otherwise glossy black hair, but her unwrinkled and unblemished face still had a glow usually found on the face of a much younger woman.

The early morning sun coming through the bedroom's only window cast a golden ray of sunlight across Ling Lee, but by design, failed to reach any of her children. Bathed in this bright sunlight, her entire upper body took on a shining celestial appearance which seemed to magically enhance her beauty.

Silently, Chi Chu's brothers and sisters entered the room.

Ling Lee, after twisting her body to the right so she better faced her children, was the first to break the silence.

"Before I speak to you of more important matters, let me tell you that no mother could ever be more proud of her children than I am of mine. Each of you has brought an equal amount of honor to the family in ways that would have filled your father's heart with pride. Because of your hard work, our family has grown from a humble beginning selling fruit from a cart, to a prosperous business known throughout Canton and beyond.

"Chung," she said as she gestured toward her second born, "because of your clever mind when dealing with the family's many and vital legal issues, our family bows to no one."

"But only because of your guidance and that of our father before you," Chung responded.

Ling Lee's hand then moved until it was pointing toward Chong.

"Chong," she said as she softly smiled. "You are my born diplomat, the angel of negotiation who has brought peace among ourselves and our competitors and ended the price wars. Your skill has kept the price of our merchandise high enough to insure a fine profit for all concerned."

"It was little that I did," was Chong's humble response.

"It was everything," said Ling Lee before fixing her eyes on her youngest son.

"Ang, your mastery of all things financial has so often protected us from the clever schemes of our competitors who would cheat us at every turn were it not for your equally clever mind."

"If I am truly clever," replied Ang, "it is a skill I learned at the side of my mother."

"Your modest words are gratefully received by that same mother," Ling Lee replied.

Her next words were directed at her daughter, the daughter whose feet she had refused to bind at birth. The daughter who could move like a butterfly caught in the wind.

"Lin Mai, my beautiful daughter," she began, "without the help and loving care you have given to your brothers and me, none of what we have accomplished as a family would have been possible. At an age when other girls are married and with a family of their own, you have sacrificed your own happiness and stayed with your undeserving…"

As his mother's voice broke from the emotion of the moment, Jose could see that her eyes were now glistening with unfallen tears. He was about to move to her side to comfort her, but as he started to rise from his chair, the quicker Lin Mai rushed past him and thrust a handkerchief into the palm of their mother's outstretched hand.

Across the room, her brothers sat in stunned silence. Never before had any of them seen their mother shed a tear or lose her composure, not even when their father had passed away.

It was as Lin Mai attended their mother, Jose, for the first time, finally noticed how closely they resembled each other. Equal in size and beauty, and as graceful of movement, they might have been taken for sisters by anyone outside the family.

Tense moments passed before Lin Mai, at her mother's insistence, returned to her chair. Moments later Ling Lee resumed talking.

"Please excuse my childish behavior," said their mother in the soft voice, "but what I am about to tell you will be as unpleasant for me to say as it is for you to hear."

After a final dab of her eyes with the handkerchief, Ling Lee continued speaking.

"For centuries, from the time of the Mongol invaders and the Khans, China has suffered at the hands of foreign invaders. Now, the British, the Japanese, and the Americans are swarming around her like vultures hovering over a dying cow. When diplomacy or meaningless treaties failed to give them everything they wanted, they used their military might to take it. They have exploited our weaknesses and turned our people into opium fed slaves to their insatiable greed. As a people, as a race, we have endured all this, as we have so many times when our country was beset by barbarians."

"That is true," said Chung, "we prevailed by either absorbing the invaders into our culture, or when it was wise to do so, through armed resistance."

"You speak of the past," said Ling Lee, "but I believe our country now faces a danger far greater than any other, and that danger will come, not from outside our country, but from within it."

Seeing the questioning look on the faces of her children, she continued.

"When I told you the danger will come from within I was referring to the centuries old civil fighting between our country's war lords. Their never ending arrogance, their refusal to combine forces has allowed other nations to keep their boots pressed to China's neck."

"So, Mother," said Jose, "what information do you have which troubles you so?"

"Reliable sources, which I have cultivated for many years, have told me that within a month the National Revolutionary Army will move from the north to here in the south. Chiang Kai-Shek intends to drive out General Bai Chongxi and claim Beijing for the NRA. If they succeed, and they will, they then intend to drive out all foreign consulates and close all of China's ports to all but a few foreign ships."

"That would mean the end of our export business and greatly decrease our assets," said Chung."

"We might survive through smuggling," replied Ling Lee, "but closing of the ports is only the beginning of the disaster which they will bring about due to their senseless intolerance of the outside world. In their infinite stupidity they also plan to create a peasant empire by punishing anyone of wealth, all intellectuals, or anyone of influence who doesn't subscribe to their political dogma. They will then seek out and punish anyone who has engaged in immoral business with, as they put it, 'imperial devils'."

"By 'punishing' you mean killing or imprisoning?" questioned Jose.

"That is a certainty," replied his mother, "and according to my source, the NRA has already compiled a long list of 'traitors to the people.' With some degree of pride I must tell you the name of Lau is high on that list."

By this time Jose understood his mother had brought them together for more than a history lesson…and knowing what he had learned of her during the months he had been back in Canton, he felt she was about to reveal her plan for the future of the family.

"Mother," he said as he gazed at his siblings and then at her, "I believe you have a plan in mind."

Ling Lee could not repress a smile as she realized that the time he had spent in Nicaragua had not diminished the superior mental capacities he had demonstrated as a youth. Contrary to her fears, he was as smart and perceptive as any of her other children, if not more so.

"You are correct," she replied to Jose, "and my plan requires that all of us make sacrifices for the good of the family, but it is from you that I must ask the greatest sacrifice."

"And one I will be honored to undertake," was Jose's immediate reply.

"You bring me great happiness with the trust you show me," she replied with a slight nod to him, "but before I speak of your role I must tell what I have done to secure your future."

A long moment passed while Ling Lee studied the face of each of her children…and saw in them the trust and strength she had hoped would be there.

"I have sold all of our holdings and assets at a price slightly below their true value, but at a price that is ten times what they will sell for in the near future. The greater part of this money has been transferred to the Hong Kong and Shanghai Banking Corporation Limited in Hong Kong. I don't think the NRA's tentacles will reach there, and why, though it breaks my heart to tell you, Hong Kong is where we make our new home."

At first, her audience met this news with a combination of both surprise and trepidation, feelings which were quickly followed by a growing sense of admiration for their mother's shrewd and swift action.

"How much time do we have?" asked Lin Mai.

It was a question Ling Lee suspected her daughter would be the one to ask. She knew her daughter had a good reason for needing to know when they would leave for Canton. For months, Ling Lee had been aware of the secret meetings between Lin Mai and a young suitor. She also knew that many of those meetings were orchestrated by her adoring brothers who were also close friends of her gentleman friend.

To Ling Lee, it was a perfect opportunity to let them know their mother was not someone they could prevent from learning even their most carefully guarded secrets.

"These old eyes are not blind to certain meetings between you and a friend of your unworthy brothers," she told them as she fought to keep a smile from her lips. "It will require at least a week to complete all of the necessary preparations. Hopefully, dear daughter, that will be enough time for you and the young man to enjoy a few more precious moments together."

While her brothers chose to say or do nothing in their defense, Lin Mai's response was to rush to her mother's side and wrap her arms about her.

"I never meant to…I…"

"Hush child," murmured Ling Lee as she wiped a tear from her daughter's cheek, "I would never question your behavior, but I must ask that you not mention anything of our plans to your friend. At a later time, after we have left Canton, I will see that he understands I have no objection to the continuation of your relationship.

"I will say nothing," promised Lin Mai before returning to her chair.

"Now, to what I must ask of Chi Chu," she told them, "life has taught me that even the best made plan may fall and crumble apart. Because of this, I must ask him to leave those who love him, and return to Nicaragua. There, I want him to build a business and

11

home of his own, one that will provide all of us a secure place to live should we need it at some future time."

After a short pause to let each of her children absorb the shock of her words, she gestured for Chi Chu to come to her bedside.

"I have made arrangements for you to return to Nicaragua beginning in two days," she told him as she took his hand in hers. "I have also had a large sum of money forwarded to the Bank of America in San Francisco. You are to use it as needed to start the business I mentioned."

Jose, as he again began thinking of himself, was tempted to mount an argument, but dismissed the thought as he began to recognize the wisdom of his mother's plan. He also realized she had placed a heavy responsibility on him, one which left him little room for argument.

"I will do as you say," he replied. "I will make a home for all of us, but even if my home is in Nicaragua, my heart will always be in China."

"Thank you," his mother replied, "and wherever I am you will always be in my heart and my prayers."

Two days later, a reluctant Jose boarded a large junk which carried him the one-hundred and twenty kilometer voyage to Hong Kong. After renting a room near the docks, he spent the rest of the day and that night in the company of a married and love starved lady he had met on board the junk. By noon of the next day, after prying himself away from his tearful companion whose name he hadn't bothered to remember, he made his way to the *Empress of China*.

Jose was still thinking of everything that had transpired during the past few days when a second blast of the ship's horn brought him back to reality. Looking toward the bow of the ship, he could see that the horn was being used to warn off a brightly colored junk which had suddenly taken up a position dangerously close to the path of the hugely larger ship. A moment later, when the bow of the *Empress* was about one-hundred yards from the junk, and perhaps fifty yards to its left, rockets began to stream from the junk's deck before bursting in a rainbow of colors above the ship.

As was true for everyone gathered about him, because of the fireworks, Jose's attention was drawn to the junk and the small group of people standing on its deck. Unknown to his fellow passengers, he was the only one who recognized who they were, and why they were there.

"They are truly amazing," was the first thought that came to his mind after he recognized them.

Just then, when they spotted him in the crowd, his entire family began waving their hands in his direction. Quite naturally, the passengers gathered around him, thinking they were the objects of his family's farewell, began to wave back.

"They certainly didn't waste any time getting out of Canton," he told himself, "but what else could I have possibly expected from them."

When the two vessels were close enough that his family could be heard over the din of the crowd, it was Chong who shouted up at him, "The deck of this junk is not a dock."

Jose had to laugh at the clever way they had stayed true to their word not to see him off from 'a dock.'

Minutes later, when the ship was freed from the tug's bonds and out of the harbor, he thought with a mixture of happiness and sadness, that "in all likelihood, I am the most blessed person on board this ship."

CHAPTER 2

March 28, 1927

The cruise from Hong Kong to Hawaii went as smoothly as any seaman could wish for. No storms, clear skies day and night, gentle seas, and with a minimum of passengers who found it necessary to chum the blue water with their latest meal.

With time on his hands, on separate occasions, Jose became a willing participant in the licentious demands of two of the more attractive and single lady passengers. Whether they had been attracted to him because of his looks, or because he had the financial means to afford a large private cabin of his own, he did not care. If they were under the illusion he was a single man of means, and therefore good husband material, who was he to correct their thinking?

Gambling, his other preferred form of entertainment, was satisfied in the ship's casino where he lost a few dollars thanks to some uncooperative dice.

On the morning of its seventh day at sea, the *Empress of China*, creeping along at one-quarter speed, followed the pilot boat into the sparkling blue water of Pearl Harbor. For most of the ship's passengers it was a first look at the port strategically located almost halfway between the Americas and the resource rich Asian mainland. Pearl Harbor, with its deep waters and isolated position making it virtually impervious to a surprise attack, was, to many military thinkers, the primary key to the control of the Pacific.

As much as anyone on board, Jose was aware of this, and therefore not at all surprised to see an impressive array of naval vessels either anchored in the harbor or berthed to a pier. Of these, the most notable, because of its enormous size and peculiar flat deck, was the carrier ship the *USS Enterprise*.

Later in the day, after passing by the battleships *Nevada* and *Arethusa*, the passengers of the *Empress* began streaming onto shore. Most of them had dedicated themselves to the task of seeing as much of the island as possible during the twelve hour layover the ship needed to take on fuel and supplies. In contrast, Jose's only goal when he stepped on shore was to enjoy a leisurely outdoor breakfast, pick up a local newspaper, have a cup or two of coffee along with a good cigar, and then take a long walk on the beach. He was to achieve only two of those goals.

Finishing his meal, Jose lit his cigar, and began to peruse the paper he'd purchased upon entering the restaurant. The lead story on the front page of the *Star Bulletin* was primarily dedicated to President Hoover's policies, Babe Ruth and the Yankees, and the legal jousting going on between the Christians and the Darwinians during the Scopes trail. Not someone to get excited about politics, sports, or religion, an unconcerned Jose turned to the other side of the page. There he found an article on the second page which sent a chill through his body.

According to the latest news to reach Hawaii, days earlier in China, a full scale civil war had broken out in the south of the country. The winning side, the

16

National Revolutionary Army, was now demanding that every foreign entity leave the country. The last few lines in the article gave only a scant mention of the loss of civilian life.

Dismayed by the possible loss of his family's home was his first reaction to the news. That feeling was quickly swept away by a sense of relief from knowing all of his family, having moved to Hong Kong before the hostilities began, were now safely under the protection of the British Lion.

That night, for the first time in a week, sleep came easily. Days later, after off-boarding in San Francisco, he would find it somewhat more difficult to get to sleep. Jose was about to discover that the coldness of the 'City by the Bay' was about to be matched by the coldness of some of its citizens.

Prejudice against the Chinese was something Jose had rarely experienced during the years he spent in Nicaragua, a country which had a long standing reputation for taking in people of different colors and cultures. During the first day of his three day layover in San Francisco, he ran head on into it.

It began when he attempted to register for a room at one of the city's upscale hotels. There, he was informed by a pompous desk clerk that we 'don't accept slant eyes.' He was met with a similar response at two other 'white only' hotels. A fourth hotel, one of a slightly lesser quality than those he had previously called on, agreed to give him a room…but only if he gave them a large enough deposit to cover the cost of unspecified 'damages.'

He settled for a modest but adequate one-dollar room in the Chinese section of town. Daily meals and a Chinese newspaper cost him an additional dollar.

Ever the obedient nephew, and adhering to the preaching of his Uncle Patricio to 'never go out in public without looking your best,' the purchase of an expensive hand tailored suit and a fashionable fedora became the only other drain on his pocket.

Days later, happy to leave San Francisco, and dressed in his new clothes, he was on a coastal steamer bound for Nicaragua.

CHAPTER 3

It was in the summer of 1931 when twenty-three year old Petrona Maria Ramos met Jose Esteban Lau, the thirty-one year old man who would become her husband.

With six brothers and five sisters, and coming from of an impoverished background, her parents and her grandfather, despite her tearful pleas to the contrary, had promised her hand in marriage to a much older man. At the time, it was a marriage arrangement not uncommon to desperately poor families with an attractive daughter. It was also an arrangement the independent minded Petrona, using lies and excuses, had managed to put off for over a year. Now, with time and excuses running out, she needed and prayed for a small miracle. It came from an unexpected source.

By this time, Jose, using the money his mother had set aside for him, had established his own mercantile and trading business in Chinandega. He had also become an excellent horseman who rode about town on a snow white stallion while wearing a matching white silk suit, with a cigar in his mouth, and a beautifully made Panama hat on head. Because of these things, he had become one of the most recognizable figures in all of the state of Chinandega. Adding to his allure, he was widely known as a dedicated womanizer, and rumored to have fathered at least one child. Given the 'macho culture' of the times, such rumors tended to increase his popularity among the men and the more 'liberally minded' ladies.

On more than one occasion Petrona had seen Jose, and wondered what it would be like to be married to someone of stature and position in the community. She also believed that for a poor and uneducated girl, with little to bring to a marriage other than a talent for cooking, to even think of rising to such a lofty position was madness.

But hope is hard to erase from the mind of the young...so she continued to have thoughts of sharing a life with him. She considered the possibility that given his reputation he might be an unfaithful husband, but she was also certain that regardless of that, being with him would be a considerable improvement over what her parents and grandfather had in mind.

"Whatever happens in the future," she told herself, "I will not accept what might be a childless life with an old man whom I could never be happy with."

Perhaps it was by chance, or perhaps it was by divine intervention, but either way, in the fading light of a spring day, Cinderella met her Prince Charming...through an entirely unplanned and unexpected act of nature.

It wasn't a major earthquake which struck the earthquake prone area that morning, just a series of tremors which were strong enough to shake the buildings and send the town's residents scurrying into the streets so as not to get caught under falling roofs. Among those who gathered in the street were Jose Lau and Petrona Maria Garcia.

She had been shopping in his store, not only to purchase needed items but also to get a glimpse of the proprietor, when the tremors began, and along with several other customers and said proprietor, had fled to safety of the center of the street. Moments later, they found themselves sitting near each other. From there, it was only natural for them to enter into a conversation.

She learned that in addition to Spanish, he also spoke Chinese, German, and English. She also discovered that he had a pleasing laugh, a soft voice...and smelled much sweeter than any other man she had ever met.

He was impressed by her simple beauty, her quiet demeanor, her infectious and perfect smile, and the calmness she showed despite the shaking ground beneath them.

After an hour had passed with no tremors, Jose and Petrona returned to the store and found it in shambles. Practically everything that had been on the shelves was on the floor. Canned goods, broken bottles, shattered glass display cases, and piles of cloth were everywhere they looked...and that was just the front of the store. More damage had been done in the storage area to the back.

Jose, seeing the mess as an opportunity to extend the time they had spent together, immediately turned to her and politely asked, "If it's not too much to ask, I'd be willing to pay you to help me clean up this mess."

Petrona hesitated for a few moments before replying, and when she did, her reply, coming from a young peasant girl, caught him by surprise.

"Would you be willing to pay me, not with money, but with merchandise from the store, and at the same price you paid for it?"

It was a clever proposition and one Jose was quick to accept. It was hours later, after they had done everything they could to put the store back together, and after Petrona had gathered her pay in several large cardboard boxes, that the enamored Jose offered her a full-time job. Her acceptance of his offer was the beginning of a romance which would lead to an affair, which, and much against her parent's wishes, led to her moving in with him.

Months later, in August of '31, either from love, lust, convenience, or a combination of the three, a somewhat unlikely couple with roots in different countries and different cultures, entered into what would become a long-lasting marriage.

The wedding, held at Our Lady Santa Ana Colonial Church and the highlight of the social year was attended by a large number of his Chinese friends and a larger number of her relatives, friends, and more than a few people who were there out of curiosity. Petrona's parents, aware of the favorable financial benefits the marriage was likely to bring to their family, happily attended the wedding. Her grandfather did not.

The following years were good ones for Jose and Petrona. Her cheerful presence in the store attracted more customers, and by working together, the store grew with each passing year. The same was true for the size of the Lau family. The first increase began in July of 1932 with the birth of Liliana. It was followed by the births of Mudra, Armando, Jaime, Alicia, and culminated with birth of Maritza.

Although life was good for the Lau's during those years, within Nicaragua difficulties abounded as different groups struggled for control of the country. At this time, the United States had a strong military and political presence in the country and for all practical purposes had made Nicaragua an American colony. The group the Americans supported was led by Anastasio Somoza Garcia, the commander of the Nicaraguan National Guard. He was smart, more politically astute than his competition, and willing to give a free rein to American companies operating in Nicaragua. He was also totally ruthless and would do anything to satisfy his power hungry ambitions, including the outright murder or torture of anyone, real or suspected, who threatened his leadership of the country.

In the early thirties, a small and poorly equipped peasant army led by seventeen year old Augusto Caesar Sandino, rose up in opposition to the U.S. presence, and against all odds, over a period of several years, forced the U.S. Marines out of the country. It was the last time a significant U.S. military force would inhabit Nicaragua. Because of his actions, Sandino became a huge national hero, an honor which was to extract a heavy price on the young hero. Seen by Somoza as a potential threat to his corrupt regime, Sandino was assassinated in 1934. Soon afterwards, in a rigged election overseen by U.S. representatives there 'to insure a fair election,' Somoza became the president of Nicaragua.

It was the start of the Somoza dynasty which would rule the country for almost half a century.

CHAPTER 4

The mid 1930's were turbulent years in much of Europe, and no more so than in and around the tiny country of Belarus, the ancestral home of the Baranovicht family. The Karl Marx inspired Socialist Party wanted to bring about a revolution dedicated to ending the feudal rule of aristocrats over the common people, and the Baranovicht family members were known to be in the upper echelon of Belarus' aristocracy.

In Germany, which had developed a massive military capability, the Nazis were rattling their sabers in the direction of Poland. The Belarusians understood that if war broke out, little land locked Belarus, which was surrounded by Poland, Latvia, Russia, Lithuania, and the Ukraine, would be helpless to prevent its destruction.

The Baranovicht family was one of hundreds of families who felt threatened by these growing clouds of war. Rather than remain in their homeland and risk losing everything, including their lives, the Baranovicht's made the heartbreaking decision to become immigrants in another land.

Joseph Baranovicht and Catilena, his Russian born wife, after brief exploratory stopovers in Honduras and Costa Rico, chose to make Nicaragua their new home. It was a wise choice. Nicaragua, under Somoza's iron rule, welcomed immigrants, especially those with money to invest…and the Baranovicht's left Belarus with enough money to invest, but for them to instantly become part of Nicaragua's growing upper middle class.

Shortly after their arrival they purchased a large swath of the fertile farm land Nicaragua was known for. It was on that land that their son Enrique was born, making him the first Baranovicht born in Nicaragua. His birth was to set the stage for the future blending together of the Lau and Baranovicht families.

With ownership of the land and the cheap labor provided by peasants, in some sense, the Baranovichts were able to create an aristocratic lifestyle similar to the one they had left behind in Belarus. Within a few years, Joseph and Catilena became part of Nicaragua's elite social and economic circle. It was a special status they would continue to enjoy as long as they expressed their unabated loyalty to the current regime by way of generous cash contributions to its ruling family.

CHAPTER 5

July 1947

During the years of World War II years when so many other countries had endured suffering and destruction on an epic scale, Nicaragua remained relatively unscathed, and even prosperous. After the deadly German U-boats were finally driven out of the Gulf of Mexico and the Caribbean, exports of Nicaraguan products, especially to the United States, reached an all-time high. Cattle, coffee, and cotton were steaming out of ports such as Managua on the Pacific coast, and Puerto Cabezas on the Gulf coast. No one reaped more from this new found prosperity than Somoza. He took the lion's share, but was astute enough to careful dispense just enough of the wealth to the military and the upper class to insure their continued support. He understood that he needed the upper class, the owners of the large farms and businesses, to keep the economy flourishing, and his bank account swelling with millions of dollars. He also made it a point to build a strong and loyal military to both protect his personal interest and the Nicaraguan borders from any intrusion by neighboring countries. Paradoxically, the massive numbers of peasants, the people who worked on the farms and ranches responsible for the agricultural bonanza, fell even deeper into poverty, misery, and starvation. The seeds of a real rebellion were being planted by an unsuspecting Somoza.

The Lau family had done well during this period. They lived in a comfortable home on the outskirts of town. The six children were happy, healthy, well-educated, and happily growing up in the midst of their mother's numerous relatives. The family's mercantile store and trading company were prosperous enough that there was little the family lacked. By Nicaraguan standards, the Lau family was well off, but not nearly to the degree of the Baranovicht family. They were rich.

That financial disparity between the two families was to undergo a huge reversal in 1947.

Petrona had been raised in unspeakable poverty. The fear of returning to that condition seldom left her mind, and was perhaps, the reason for her being as frugal as she was. To her everlasting consternation, much of what she was able to save her husband managed to lose by gambling on slow horses and cock-fights, but above all, the National Lottery. Overnight, it could make a lucky winner rich beyond his dreams. And if anything, Jose was a dreamer.

Although she would occasionally criticize him about the money he lost at the track or the cock fighting rings, she never berated him about the money he spent on the lottery. She knew how important it was for him to nourish his dream of winning the lottery...and she knew why.

Correspondence between Jose and his family in Hong Kong had been almost nonexistent during the war years. A single letter had reached him in 1945, but said little other than to inquire about the welfare of his family. It said nothing about conditions in Hong Kong or his mother's and sibling's welfare. To Jose, who felt his family didn't want to worry him with bad news, this did not bode well. A month after the Japanese signed the surrender agreement aboard the battleship *Missouri*, two letters postmarked two months apart, arrived on the same day. To relief, the first letter, which he opened with trembling fingers, written by his mother, spoke only of family matters and her hope that all was well with his Nicaraguan family. The second letter, written by Lin Mai, tore at his heart and brought him to tears. Her letter informed him that their mother, who was approaching seventy, was very ill with only months to live at best. He also learned that his mother, when she realized she was approaching the end of her life, had made two requests of her children.

"When it is safe to do so," she told them, "before I die, I want you to take me back to Canton so that I can be buried next to your father."

Her other request was more of a wish, that wish being that she could see Chi Chu for one last time.

The last part of the letter told him that "my brothers have arranged to take our mother home within a week or two, but I fear that Canton is still a dangerous city. Because of this, despite my love and respect for our mother, I have made the painful decision to remain in Hong Kong with my husband and family."

After Jose had composed himself enough to translate the contents of the letter to his wife and children, only Petrona suspected how close they were to losing him. It was no secret to her that her husband had always intended, as he often put it, 'to return home to my Chinese family.'

Only the war in the Pacific during the time that they were creating their own family had kept him from leaving Nicaragua...and that war was over.

Lady Luck can be a capricious mistress. She can give with one hand, and without any warning, take with the other. For the Lau's, this was to be what happened in the days after Jose had received the two letters from Hong Kong. It began with an enormous blessing, a blessing which would soon turn into a dreadful curse...and lend support to the age old proverb that 'money is the source of all evil.'

A month after receiving the letters, Jose's habitual gambling on the National Lottery paid off in a gigantic way. Against odds of millions to one, he won, and won big, well over a hundred thousand dollars. This windfall was the answer to his dreams of returning to Canton. To Petrona, it was the beginning of a nightmare which would last for decades to come.

"When we get the money from the lottery," Jose announced to her in a tone of voice which suggested there was no room for argument on her part, "we are all going home to Canton."

Petrona, like any mother upon hearing her children might be placed in danger, was having none of it.

"That's fine for you," she snapped back with no attempt to hide her anger, "in China, you would have your precious family, but myself and the children would have nothing. No friends, no family, nothing, nothing, and more nothing."

"I love you and our children, but I have to go," he responded apologetically, "it is my duty as a son."

"And it is my duty to protect our children by keeping them here with my family, and not in a country that is totally strange to them and to me."

It was at that moment he realized that because of their loyalty to their families, both of them were caught squarely between the proverbial 'rock and a hard place,' and a fight which neither one of them could win, wasn't the answer. They had to reach some sort of compromise.

A week later, that compromise, which did not fully satisfy either of them, was reached. Jose, along with four of his children, and with half of the winnings from the lottery, was aboard a ship heading out of Managua and bound for China. He left behind his wife, their son Jaime, and Maritza, their two-year old daughter. Contrary to most traditions of that time, in the will he left behind, it was the infant daughter, and not the older brother who had run away to avoid going with his father, who was named as the beneficiary to the remaining Lau fortune.

In a tragic twist of fate, it would be the last time the Lau family would be together. Neither Jose, nor any of the four children, was ever heard from again. China, that enormous bastion of chaos, mystery, and unrest, had swallowed up the Laus as easily as a river would swallow a handful of pebbles dropped in it.

Over the years, Petrona and Jose's sister Lin Mai repeatedly inquired to numerous authorities in the Americas and China about the fate of the missing Laus. All attempts on their part proved to be futile.

Petrona, along with Jaime and Maritza, continued the family businesses and the Lau fortune continued to grow. Their monetary good fortune allowed them to occasionally mix in the same social circles the Baranovicht's had become part of after immigrating to Nicaragua. It was during one of these occasions that Enrique became infatuated with the beautiful Maritza. Not long afterwards they began a courtship.

In late 1967, Enrique Baranovicht and the strikingly beautiful twenty-two year old Maritza Lau were married in a lavish wedding attended by hundreds of people at the same church her parents had been married in thirty-six years earlier. During the ensuing years, they would become parents to three children, Salvador, Moises, and Yahel. As the three children grew into their teen years, they were destined to become both witnesses and victims to the bloody civil war which was about to engulf the entire country.

CHAPTER 6

In the 1960's, the Sandinistas, also known as the FSLN, were few in number and composed mainly of peasants and a few patriotic leaders, some of whom had professional backgrounds such as business, education, and the clergy. They conducted a guerilla style war in the mountains and jungles, emerging only long enough to make 'hit and run attacks' before melting back into the remote areas of the country. Or, when pursued by the numerical superior and better armed National Guard, crossing into Honduras. They had little in the way of arms or money, with only a meager outside source of support coming from Cuba and the Soviets. It wasn't much, but it was enough to keep them going, and make them a thorn in the side of the Somoza regime.

On paper, Somoza's National Guard and the army had every advantage. They outnumbered the rebels as much as five to one. The army, which did most of the real fighting, had more men and more arms, including attack helicopters and up to date weapons and modern communication equipment supplied by the United States government. It was David against Goliath, and David didn't have much in the way of a sling shot.

The lesson the over confident Somoza and his supporters in the United States government had yet to learn was that a war isn't fought on paper. Wars are fought on the battlefield and in the heart. And the best soldiers are those willing to die for a cause they believe in. In that respect, Somoza's forces had several serious weaknesses when it came to waging war, especially in the remote mountains surrounded by dense jungles.

For the most part, the army was made up of conscripted peasants who were poorly paid and had little enthusiasm for fighting against their own people, people from their own lower class. People they may have been friends of, or as often occurs in a civil war, people they were related to.

Their training made them more of an urban police force rather than a battlefield ready army. They were reasonably, if not brutally proficient, at controlling non-violent dissidents such as college students, political opponents, unarmed peasants, and anyone else even mildly opposed to Somoza. However, when they left the cities, when they left their armored vehicles, when they went into unfamiliar jungle and mountains, the Sandinistas held the advantage. Not only did the army exhaust themselves trying to chase down the elusive Sandinistas, when they were able to find and engage them, it was like hunters catching up with an elusive tiger and then getting severely mauled for their success.

To the Sandinistas, the jungle was both their home and their green fortress. After twenty years of fighting and living in the jungle, they knew every trail, every stream, every hiding place, and where the best sites to carry out their deadly ambushes. They had become superb and highly dedicated guerrilla fighters.

The army was none of these things.

By the mid-seventies the war was going badly for the Somoza family. The Sandinistas, now better equipped thanks to increased aid from the Russians and the Cubans, could be counted in the thousands, and had taken the fight to Somoza with surprising successes. Worried that he was losing ground to the increasingly popular Sandinistas, a desperate Somoza called for more aid from the United States, the same United States which had already supplied him with vast amounts of cash and materials.

The Carter and Reagan administrations, ensconced in the Cold War and paranoid about losing Central America to communism, were caught in a political trap which Somoza used to his advantage. He knew the Sandinistas, who strongly advocated communism, gave the leaders of the United States few options from which to choose. First, they could simply do nothing, which would allow the communists to take over Nicaragua, and possibly set in motion the dreaded 'domino effect' which would bring other Central American countries toppling into the communist fold. That was not acceptable, either militarily, politically, or economically, to the leaders of the United States. They couldn't afford another Cuban fiasco…and they certainly didn't want to lose the support of fruit companies whose generous contributions kept them in office and increasingly wealthy.

Their second option was to more openly support a brutal self-serving dictator whose atrocities against his own people were already being exposed to the public by the news media and human rights organization around the world. With the American voters inherently opposed to dictators, but brainwashed into fearing communism, such open support of Somoza was political suicide. The U.S. was able to choose between the 'lesser of two evils,' and to both administrations, Somoza was considered the lesser of the two.

Once again, the more politically astute Somoza had perfectly outplayed and out maneuvered both the former actor and the Georgia farmer.

CHAPTER 7

The unmarked C130 cargo plane touched down on the tarmac of Managua's airport at 0300 hours. Seconds after the plane taxied to a stop two-hundred meters from a darkened hanger set away from the main terminal, six men dressed in ordinary clothes, exited the plane. They were quickly followed by six duffel bags handed down to them by the plane's co-pilot.

To the casual eye, the six men might have seemed to be unarmed, but that was far from being true. Concealed beneath their jackets, and in the duffle bags, was a lethal assortment of weapons. After seeing three blinks of a vehicle's parking lights coming from the side of the hanger, the men picked up their duffle bags in one hand and started walking in the direction of the lights. Their other hand was left empty, but poised only inches away from a handgun, or in one case, a sawed off shotgun. None of the men expected trouble, but being prepared for the unexpected was an essential part of their existence.

By the time the men reached the truck, the plane which had never shut down its engines, was back in the air and disappearing into the night sky.

If someone had searched them, no means of identifying any of the plane's former passengers would have been found. To the outside world, they were nameless. They were also extremely lethal, ultra-secretive, and among the best fighting men to come out of the Viet Nam war. Days before, after being told that their mission was to go to Nicaragua and train

Somoza's regular army, their superiors in Virginia had designated them 'the Alpha Team.'

"Hustle it up," said the first man to reach the truck. "We need to get out of the city and reach the army camp before daylight."

The country-sounding man giving the orders was former Army Sergeant Jerry Waller, a muscular, six-foot five farm boy from the small town of Lively Grove, Illinois. To the men he was closest he was 'Abner,' the nickname given to him in Vietnam by his first squad leader as a tribute to his size fourteen brogans.

"I'll be upfront keeping an eye on the driver," said Abner to the others.

"He wouldn't be in such a hurry if he knew Managua like I do," said the man they called Lobo. "She has the most beautiful women in all of Central America."

The speaker had the given name was Eduardo Jorge Sanchez, born outside Chinandega, and was the only native Nicaraguan on the team. Although all of the men of the Alpha team spoke reasonable Spanish, he was their designated interpreter.

"And the ugliest men," responded the lanky black man standing to Lobo's left. His name was Leonard Parker, but he preferred being called 'Poochie,' the name his family had attached to him shortly after he was born. Lean and fun loving, he had exceptional hand eye coordination and a penchant for working with explosives. Before joining the army, he had been a nationally ranked track star in high school. He was also Lobo's closest friend.

"I hope you two lovebirds don't plan on chirping the night away because I plan to get some sleep," muttered a voice from the rear of the truck.

The disgruntled voice belonged to Steven 'Slim' Smith, a Houstonian with a degree from Texas A and M. An outdoorsman by nature and something of a loner, he spent much of his free time mountain climbing, spelunking, and scuba diving. His adventurous spirit did not include flying. Comfortable in any other environment, he had a serious fear of flying, and was the only one of the team who had been unable to sleep during the long hours they had spent in the air.

Standing silently, Willie Lessert, the team's radio operator and medic, was the fifth man to climb into the truck. Born in North Dakota, and a native Indian, he was the only member of the team who might have been described as quiet, or even sullen. Although intensely proud of his heritage, starting in boot camp, some misguided people had learned the hard way that he didn't appreciate being addressed as 'Chief.'

The last man to climb into the truck was Ron Hall, an Ohioan from Dayton with a talent for throwing a knife. He and the 'Sarge' had been like brothers since boot camp and all during their time in 'Nam. Bull strong and with a strong dislike of authority uncommon to most soldiers, he, never-the-less, preferred the action of a fighting man to that of a civilian. By always watching the other's back, he and Abner had kept themselves alive during some of the bloodiest battles of the war.   Wells, primarily by using his homemade knife and a 45 caliber pistol he'd taken from a Viet Cong soldier.

Before any more verbal darts could be tossed around, the truck's engine belched to a start. As the truck got underway, the driver lit a cigarette and passed the pack and a book of matches to his passenger.

"Thanks," said Abner after lighting a cigarette and blowing out a lung full of smoke.

"I'm Carlos," replied the driver as Abner handed back the cigarette and matches.

"I know," said Abner, "I read your file. Special Ops, some of it wet. It was impressive for...a jarhead."

"Abner, ol' buddy, it might have been more impressive if us Marines hadn't spent so much time getting your sorry Army butts out of a jam."

Carlos's use of his name told Abner he wasn't the only one who had read a file.

"What are we looking at in the army camp?" asked Abner.

"SNAFU at its finest level," replied Carlos, "bad food, no discipline, electricity sometimes, and no hot water for showering. If I was you, I'd stock up on some of the local brew, because you don't want to drink the water unless you like having the trots for days at a time."

"Sounds lovely," replied Abner as he recalled the trots he had endured during his two tours in 'Nam.

"And you'll love this," said Carlos. "There are some sorry ass junior officers in the camp, but the last time I looked, there was no higher ranking officer in charge."

"You're telling me there's no one in command?"

"The higher ranking officers are a bunch of asses. They know why you and your men are here," replied Carlos, "and didn't want anything to do with that kind of training. My guess is they haven't had a real CO in weeks, maybe even longer."

"Sounds sweet," said Abner, "maybe we won't have to start out by fracking somebody."

"Ooh rah to that," said Carlos as he turned left and to the north in the direction of Chinandega.

Two hours later, and after passing through the narrow unlit streets of Chinandega, the truck left the asphalt road and turned right on to a spine jarring dirt road. An hour later, after Carlos waved his ID at the two guards manning the open gate, the truck passed through the lightly guarded front gate of the army camp."

To Abner, the camp looked about as military as a hippy compound. Sagging canvas tents were scattered about in no real order. A single guard tower stood unmanned and poorly positioned. A small tanker truck was parked off to one side with jerry cans scattered about it. A rusty tin building with a broken antennae protruding from the roof looked like the communication center. A dirty white building with rolled up canvas stretchers leaning against it appeared to be the infirmary. Two dogs digging through a pile of trash next to a mess tent completed the disorderly picture.

Like Abner, the five men inside the truck had reached what amounted to the same negative opinion of what they were seeing.

"Not too bad," said a sarcastic Ron, "a terrific looking communications center, an outdoor cafe, a complete medical facility, a bustling service station, and best of all, a canine corps ready to ward off the bad guys."

"And on two sides, only a few hundred yards separating the perimeter of this so called camp, from a big patch of jungle," said Lobo.

"The Three Stooges with sling shots could take this place in less time than it takes me to piss," replied Slim.

On the far side of the camp, the driver stopped the truck in front of the only well maintained structure the men had observed. When everyone was out of the truck, a grinning Carlos informed them, "Welcome to your new home away from home."

To the men of the Alpha team, it was also an instant mystery as to why it was there. It was an American made mobile home which looked to be about 60x14 feet in size, and had no reason any of the team could think of for being there.

"Why?" asked Ron who was speaking for the others, "would anyone go to the considerable expense to have a trailer shipped all the way from the U.S. to Nicaragua."

The mystery was explained to them by Carlos.

"A trailer is the best place to be during an earthquake," he told them, "because it sits on tires and will shake during an earthquake, but is unlikely to collapse or even be damaged like a rigid structure built on the ground."

He went on to explain that it was air conditioned, had its own generator, fully furnished, and had been the property of a local landowner until one of the prior commanders of the camp 'requisitioned' it for his own use.

"I wonder, who's the officer in charge of this pig sty?" commented Ron as he approached the trailer's small porch.

"My money says it's a joint command between the two dogs digging in the trash," quipped Slim.

"Not a chance," relied Ron, "they were working too hard to be officers."

Abner didn't bother telling them that the camp was without a commander, and they were both wrong. An hour later, after putting away their gear and eating breakfast style MREs, they woke up the camp and assembled all of its inhabitants in front of the trailer's porch.

The team had been assigned to join the army as 'advisors,' and given the nearly impossible job of training as many of the Nicaraguans as possible in only four weeks. Given that the Alpha Team's presence in Nicaragua was best left out of the media and without the approval of Congress; they were also ordered to do this without drawing any undue attention to themselves. The last thing they were instructed to do by their boss was to 'make damn sure you avoid shooting anyone.'

"Based on what I'm seeing," said Ron as he looked at the men standing casually in front of him, "I think we're about three months short of the time we need to train these guys."

"I think that's the same thing our DI said about us back in the day," replied Abner, "and look at how that worked out."

"Yeah, and that's why I'm worried."

They spent the first three days weeding out the lost causes from the men who might be capable of being turned into decent soldiers. Of the first sixty-four 'volunteers' that had been assigned to the camp, fifty-six survived the initial cut. By the fifth day that number had been reduced to forty-eight. All of the soldiers who had failed to make the cut were put to work getting the camp in order. Their labor inspired the others to greater efforts. The four junior officers, after expressing their disapproval of their treatment and threatening to report the American's behavior to the Somozas, were invited to leave the camp. All of them accepted the invitation.

To the six Americans who gathered together each night to review the day's events, it was a dismal beginning.

"Can you believe these people call themselves soldiers?" questioned Ron, a man who believed in a lot of spit and polish as long as it applied to someone else.

"Give 'em a break," Lobo responded. "Most of them were peasants who were either drafted right off the farm or joined up because it was the only work available to them. Very few of them got past the sixth grade or ever held a weapon unless it was a pitchfork or a machete used in the sugar cane fields."

"I've seen girl scouts in better shape," said Slim. "On her worst day my mama could outrun half of them."

"It's a good thing she couldn't outrun the milkman," said Lobo, but then dodged any reply from Slim by adding, "but you've got to remember, they get paid almost nothing, not to mention that they've had jokes for officers. Most likely, they bought their commissions rather than earning them."

"Whatever their problems are," said Abner, "they're our problems now, and we've got damn little time to get these guys shaped up."

The training of the remaining soldiers began with six days a week of hard core training. Mornings began with intense conditioning exercises designed to prepare the troops for the physical hardships of real combat. The afternoons and early evenings were dedicated to arms training and how to conduct basic military operations, such as using hand signals when communicating. The men were given Sundays off, partly to allow them time to recover from their aches and injuries, but mostly because there was no way to keep them from attending church services held by a visiting priest from Chinandega. On those Sunday afternoons, to keep them busy and out of trouble, after the church services ended, the soldiers were given the option of either playing a game of six-man soccer against the Americans or watching a worn out John Wayne movie. To the cheering of their fellow soldiers, the slower Americans were narrowly defeated by the Nicaraguans. After one game was over, a frustrated Lobo accused the other team of being 'a bunch of ringers.' As it turned out, losing the game had lightened his money clip by several twenty-dollar bills.

At the beginning of the next week, the timing of the training was switched around. The extensive arms training began in the morning and lasted until noon followed by conditioning exercises during the heat of the afternoon. Then came hand-to-hand combat and evening sessions of studying maps, basic first aid, land to air communications, and the understanding of guerilla tactics.

The third week was devoted to implementing 'the four commandments of jungle warfare' that had been learned in Viet Nam. To make the commandments easier for the men to remember, they were referred to as the four S's. Those four S's were also printed and then posted on the inside of the latrine stalls. They read:

Silence: Look where you're stepping before you step. The sound of a footfall or a breaking branch could be answered with gunfire. Use hand signals during the day, touching at night. Stay quiet at all times.

Stealth: Move slowly. Use as much cover as possible. Day or night, stop every few feet to look and listen. Never leave anything behind that might alert the enemy to your presence. No smoking. Avoid breaking branches. Never use the same path twice.

Shine: Never wear or carry anything that can reflect the sunlight or the moonlight. Use grease or dirt on your face and weapons. Use whatever materials are available to make yourself one with your surroundings.

Shape: There are few straight or round objects in nature. Position yourself in a way that breaks up such lines or shapes. Don't make a silhouette of yourself because that can make you a target.

The final phase of the training was the litmus test for instructors and soldiers alike. It was time for a two day long mock exercise that would put what they had been taught, and what had been learned, to the test.

Four members of the Alpha team would act as the guerillas, and would be given a six hour head start. The soldiers, formed into eight man squads, were given the job they had been training for. They had to 'seek, find, and then destroy' the enemy in as little time as possible with a minimum number of casualties. Abner and Ron would remain behind with the soldiers, but not in an advisory capacity. Their job was to act as observers, moving from squad to squad to evaluate the men's performance, and lastly, to determine if any of the men demonstrated the intelligence and leadership needed to become an officer. Good officers would be essential to the future success of the Nicaraguan army.

Over the two days and nights of the exercise, to the dismay of their instructors, the soldiers performed even more poorly than expected. What they did, or didn't do, wasn't a full- fledged disaster, but it came close. On the first day, two of the scouts assigned to the point position for their squads, failed to notice obvious signs deliberately left behind by 'the enemy.' The next two scouts were doing better until they got too far ahead and became temporarily lost and separated from their squad. The smell of burning tobacco often lingered in the areas the squads passed through. Because of this, two of the squads were 'wiped out' in a series of ambushes, stepped on fake personal mines, and set off booby traps a sharp-eyed child could have avoided. One of the squads which walked into the first ambush even managed to walk blindly into a second and more obvious ambush.

The single saving grace coming out of the exercise was that only three men were injured. One man in a squatting position was bit by a snake on his tail end, a second man stabbed himself through the hand while opening a can of Spam, and a third soldier cracked a kneecap on a rock when he fell down an embankment.

As bad as the exercise had gone, it had produced a favorable change in the attitude of the soldiers. After a thorough review of their performance, the men, most of whom had been complacent about their initial training, began to understand how much they needed to learn if they were to survive future engagements with the more experienced Sandinistas. It was a rude awakening and it dramatically changed their attitude toward training.

It was impossible for the members of the Alpha team not to feel responsible for the men they were training. On the other side of the coin, the Nicaraguan soldiers, who had at first been skeptical of the Americans, were slowly beginning to trust them. It was the kind of bonding that is often formed when men, even from radically different cultures, live and train under the shadow of warfare.

A day after the exercise had ended, when the Nicaragua soldiers approached the Americans and pleaded for additional and more extensive training, the Alpha team, after sending a coded message to Langley, received permission to remain in the country for an additional month.

"It's a good thing they said yes," Lobo told the others, "because I wasn't going anywhere until we'd done what we came here to do."

Willie spoke for the other men when he responded, "You wouldn't have been alone."

"Can you imagine?" replied Abner, "us having to admit to the suits that we'd been lost in the jungle for a month."

"Who would of *thunk* it," replied a smiling Poochie.

"What I *thunk*," said Abner, "is that we all better get some sleep because tomorrow is a whole new ball game."

CHAPTER 8

Before the sun was up the following morning, training began in earnest, and the Nicaraguans, whom Abner now described as 'our men,' were showing a new found dedication. With the basic training already out of the way, the emphases shifted to other, more specialized training. It began with tougher conditioning exercises, including an obstacle course which demanded a higher degree of personal effort and team cooperation. That was followed by hours of practice at hand-to-hand fighting, judo, and bayonet drills. Under the critical eye of the Alpha team, the men learned how to take apart, clean, and then reassemble and fire every caliber of weapon available to them or the enemy. These weapons included a light weight machine gun and an RPG taken from the duffle bags. Making it even tougher, all the drills, all the exercises, everything they were asked to do in the daytime, they had to repeat in the dark of night.

In the afternoon of the ninth day of training, the men were ready to begin their daily five mile run, but were interrupted when two trucks and a car carrying four men in uniform, rolled past the front gate and pulled to a stop in front of the guards. A minute later, the car and the trucks came to a halt before the assembled men. Nothing about the unmarked car gave a clue to its passengers' identities, but the trucks were clearly marked in bold white letters, Nicaraguan National Guard.

"What do you suppose these guys want?" Poochie asked Abner. "Because I don't remember us sending anyone an invitation."

"I do believe they come bearing gifts," Abner replied.

He didn't bother to tell Poochie that the trucks were probably filled with 'a few supplies' he had asked Langley to send ASAP. His reason for not telling anyone of the shipment was his awareness that much of the money and aid the U.S. sent to help the Somoza government combat the communists, had a habit of disappearing or ending up in one of the Somozas' Swiss bank accounts. If that was to happen to the things he had requested, Abner didn't want anybody but himself to be disappointed.

The four men in the car and two of the Americans met in front of the nearby ranks of the curious and apprehensive troops. To a man, the troops had learned from past experience that the unannounced arrival of any of Somoza's notorious National Guard, whether it was four or forty of them, usually meant big trouble for some unlucky soul.

Three of the men who exited the car were ordinary looking and low ranking soldiers. The fourth man, and the shortest of the four, was dressed more in keeping with a parade ground than a remote training base. To the two Americans whom he approached, it was a case of instant dislike.

"I am Captain Quintero, your new Commandant," announced the visitor with a snappy salute that went unanswered.

After waiting for a moment to have his salute returned by the two men standing before him, he lowered his hand. The slight smile on his face changed to a tight lipped grimace.

"I have brought you the supplies you requested," he told them, "but I must also inform you that we have orders to remain with you as observers until the training of my men has been completed."

"The trucks can stay," replied Abner, "but we have no need for observers, regardless of your rank or orders."

"But I must insist," said Quintero in a smug manner dripping with self- importance.

He had noticed that neither of the Americans was armed. It was an omission on their part that he wouldn't hesitate to use to his advantage.

"And I insist that you leave. Now," replied Abner.

"Then you leave me no choice," replied Quintero as he nodded toward the soldiers standing behind him and unsnapped the cover of his pistol, "but to…"

"But to do as the man says, Senor. Get back in the car and haul your asses out of here."

The voice came from behind Quintero and his men. When he turned to look, he saw four dangerous looking men, and unlike the other Americans standing in front of him, they were very much armed. Two of them were holding automatic pistols aimed at his men. Another had an M16 cradled in his arms. The fourth man had a short barreled shotgun pointed in his direction. Quintero also realized the men holding the weapons were close enough that there was little possibility of them missing their target…and he was that target.

What Quintero could not hide from the men watching the armed confrontation was that he was visibly shaking. It was obvious his pompous arrogance had melted away. He'd gone from being the cock of the walk to a frightened banty rooster. He had his orders, and he knew what often happened to officers who sometimes failed to carry out even the most inconsequential orders from El Presidentè. But of even greater concern to him at that moment, he was also aware of the kind of damage a shot gun could inflict at close range.

"I…I," he stammered.

"Now," Abner told him, "and leave your weapons on the ground."

A minute later, the car, now crammed with four men and the truck drivers, was churning up a cloud of dust as it went speeding away from the camp.

To the troops who had cheered the departure of the National Guard soldiers, the Alpha team had become six heroes they were ready to follow, as one of them put it, 'to hell and back.'

Their admiration for the Americans increased even more when they discovered the first truck was filled back to front with new up-to-date weapons. To their greater delight, they soon discovered that the second truck was loaded with fresh food straight from the best markets and butcher shops in Managua. They almost choked from laughing when they found a requisition stamped with For National Guard Use Only.

All of the Alpha team agreed with their men when they claimed 'now the food will taste even better.'

For the following two weeks the training was relentless, but in the eyes of both the Americans and the men, it was paying off. The extra rations from the truck and the hard physical training had added much needed strength and stamina to every man. They were becoming the physically fit and hard core soldiers their instructors wanted them to be. But how they would respond to actual combat was a question which would remain unanswered until two weeks later.

Days before that time came, Lobo announced to the other members of the Alpha team, "On Sunday, I'm taking a truck into Chinandega to see some people I used to know. If any of you want to tag along with me, feel free to join me."

The following afternoon, Abner was the truck's lone passenger. The other members of the team had chosen to stay behind to play double-deck Pinochle for what they described as "the championship of the universe."

When Lobo and Abner were a few miles from Chinandega, and after passing large herds of cattle grazing in fields of lush grass, along with endless rows of cotton plants and shoulder high cornstalks, Abner drawled, "This is about the best looking farmland I've ever seen... except of course for the farm country of southern Illinois."

"That's because erupting volcanos have been dumping ash deposits in this area for thousands of year," said Lobo, "making it the best soil in the world…except for southern Illinois of course."

"With dirt like this, I'd expect to see more farmhouses," said Abner, "but they seem to be few and far between."

"You don't see the farm houses because very few peasants own the land. Most of the good farmland is owned by large companies who operate at the discretion of the Somoza family, and the rest of the land, maybe as much as twenty-five percent, is owned by the Somoza family."

"It's good to be the big dog." said Abner.

"It's been that way clear back to the time of the Mayans," replied Lobo.

At that moment, they passed a line of people who, by their simple clothes and the tools they were carrying, had to be peasant farm workers. To Abner's distain, most of them were young frail looking children.

"Those are kids," said Abner. "Not just working but working on Sunday?"

"Yeah, they are just kids," replied Lobo, "and they're working the fields on Sunday from an early age because they have to if they want something to eat on Monday," replied Lobo, "and twenty years ago, I would have been one of those kids."

Abner was surprised to hear about an unknown part of Lobo's life. He had always known that Lobo was born in Nicaragua, but had assumed, because of his stories about his schooling, playing American football, and Lobo's lack of an accent, that he came to the states when he was a baby. Added to that, men in combat, with the threat of dying looming over them, form deep bonds and trusting relationships seldom found anywhere else, even among families. In the telling of their lives, it's rare that anything significant goes unsaid.

"You were one of them…a farm worker?"

"Yep," answered Lobo as he started to slow the truck. "Me and my whole family, and if you look to the right you'll be looking at our old house."

Abner looked, and could see a small and dilapidated house sitting in the middle of a bare patch of dirt. Scattered about the yard were several wash tubs, some wooden chairs, a rusted out pick-up truck with its hood up, and what looked like rabbit cages. The only things moving were several chickens scratching in the dirt, and some clothes hanging over a clothes line stretched between two small trees.

"Has it changed much?" asked Abner.

"If you mean the house, it seems smaller," replied Lobo with a shake of his head, "but if you meant the work, no, it never changes unless it's for the worse."

Nothing more was said until they reached the town and Lobo parked the truck in front of a building with a sign which read *LAU'S MARKET*.

"Grocery shopping?" asked Abner, "you hoping to score some Twinkies?"

"Better than that," replied Lobo, "I'm hoping to see some old friends of my family."

When they entered through the screen door, the store was empty except for a gray cat lounging on the counter next to a small hand bell. Abner rang the bell with one hand while rubbing the cat's head with the other. Seconds later, a woman with flour covered hands, emerged from the back of the store and made her way behind the counter.

"Can I help you," she asked as she wiped her hands on the apron tied around her waist."

"I'm looking for Senora Petrona Lau," said Lobo, "years ago, she was a friend to my mother."

"I am Petrona," replied the woman, "and I hope I am still a friend to your mother, whoever she might be."

"I am Edwardo Sanchez. My mother's name was Elena."

"It is a name I have not heard in many years, and it's true, we were very good friends…and how is your mother?"

"She is well, and living in Texas, near San Marcos," replied Lobo, "she still speaks of you as her angel because of the food you gave her for our family. She asked, if I found you, that I thank you for your kindness."

"It was nothing," Petrona replied, "but now, look at you all grown into a man, and here with the Americans."

"You know us?" asked Abner.

Petrona hesitated for a moment before replying. Ordinarily she would have been too cautious to reveal the extent of her knowledge, but because the man accompanied Lobo, she replied, "There are many eyes and ears in Chinandega, so yes, I know who you are. Everyone in Chinandega knows about the Americans who are training the army."

"It's nice to be noticed," said Abner, but thinking quite the opposite.

He might have said more, but was interrupted by a woman and a small boy entering the store. Despite the woman's obvious pregnancy, Abner thought she bore a strong resemblance to the woman behind the counter.

"This is my daughter Maritza and my grandson, Salvador," announced Petrona with more than a small amount of pride. She than added, "Maritza, these two gentlemen are Edwardo Sanchez and his American friend, Sergeant Waller."

It took only seconds for Abner to realize she knew his name, even though he had not been introduced to her. It was a disturbing thought that the veil of secrecy he had hoped to maintain had been so easily ripped away in such a short amount of time.

"The town may have big ears and eyes," he thought, "and some of the men must have even bigger mouths."

"Hello," said Maritza as she patted her stomach, "and this is little Moises."

Abner was beginning to like both of these pleasant and unpretentious women. It occurred to him that they and the store reminded him of the general store run by his relatives back home in Lively Grove.

"Please to meet both of you," replied Abner as he gave a slight bow while looking in the direction of the young lady's protruding stomach.

"And Moises is pleased to meet the brave men who ran off Captain Quintero," she replied, "and so too is his mother and grandmother."

Abner, hearing Maritza speak of Quintero, couldn't hide the look of surprise on his face.

"Don't be so surprised," said Petrona when she saw the look on the American's face, "after his meeting with you, he stopped in the store to make a phone call."

"We heard everything," added Maritza, "and it didn't sound like the people on the other end of the line were very happy with our poor Captain Quintero."

"*Our* Captain Quintero," said Abner, "so I guess you're on Somoza's side and not that of the Sandinistas."

"We try our best not to take either side," replied Petrona, "it helps that the Sandinistas think of us as little more than peasants, while the government sees us not being prosperous enough to be of any real value to them."

"So," said Lobo, "you get ignored by both sides."

An hour later, as Lobo and Abner were about to leave the store with a bag full of deep fried tajadas and several boxes of cigars, Petrona stopped them.

"You should know that Quintero is not a forgiving man. He will seek to punish you because of the trouble you caused him," she warned, "but the Sandinistas are much more dangerous. They have been watching you. They know who you are, and they know why you're here, so please be careful."

On the way back to camp, Abner and Lobo started discussing what they had learned, and what it might mean to their mission. It was clear to both men that Petrona's words should be taken as a serious warning.

"What would you do?" asked Abner, "if you were the Sandinistas and knew we were here, and that we pose a threat to you."

"I'd hit that threat, probably at night, and I'd hit it hard," said Lobo.

"So would I," replied Abner, "and right now I think we've been living lucky and living on borrowed time."

"And it's time for us to flee or fight," Lobo responded, "and I'm dammed sure tired of us not doing what we do best."

"Well," said Abner as he passed a cigar to Lobo, "so much for those orders about us not getting directly involved with the Sandinistas."

Lobo knew exactly what his friend had on his mind. Abner was already thinking of how to go on the offensive and hit the enemy before he hit them.

"Time to rock and roll?" asked Lobo.

"Time for us to have a little fun," replied Abner.

As the truck turned on to the dirt road leading to the camp, both men had contented looks on their face as they leisurely puffed on their cigars. When they got back to camp and explained to the men their plans to take the fight to the Sandinistas, all but a few of the cigars got passed out.

CHAPTER 9

That night the Americans sat down to work out the details of the plan. When that was completed, Lobo was selected to tell the troops what was planned for them. The next morning, the men were assembled, and the plan was laid out for them. After Lobo finished filling them in, all of the men were eager to go after the Sandinistas, but half of them were more than unhappy when they heard that they were to be left behind.

"I can understand your wanting to go on the raid," said Lobo, "but we need you to stay here, to protect the camp and make it appear as if all of us are here. We know our presence here is known by the Sandinistas. If we can fool them into believing all of us are still here, the less likely they are to think we have gone on the attack. If they suspect that, it could seriously endanger our chances of surprising them. It could also mean that most likely we would be walking into a trap."

At that point it was the longest speech that Lobo had ever given, but he wasn't done. He had one more card to play. It was a card the Americans hoped would bolster the troops' fighting spirit.

"During the war in Viet Nam, me and the Americans standing here with me, served together in the army. We were Bravo Company, 9th Infantry Regiment, 25th Infantry Division, and we were bad asses to the bone. We were the real thing, warriors who were bloodied in some of the worst battles of the war. Because of our toughness, and because of how hard we fought, we became known as the Manchus, the best of the best. We were feared and respected by our allies and enemies alike. We were proud to be called the Manchus. Today, as we prepare to go into combat with you, we ask that you honor us by allowing us to call you Manchus."

To a man, and in concert with the Americans, the army began shouting, "Manchus. Manchus. Manchus."

The twenty-one men selected to go on the raid were split up into three squads, designated Blue, White, and Triangle, representative of the colors and symbol of the Nicaraguan flag. Abner, along with Willie, would be in charge of the Triangle squad. Lobo and Poochie got the White squad. Slim and Ron headed up the Blue squad.

Each member of each squad would have a specific job to carry out. Three men would be in charge of the M60 machine gun. It could go through a belt full of 7.62 caliber rounds in seconds. This meant one man would carry and then man the M60, and the other two men would carry four or more of the heavy ammo belts holding one-hundred rounds each.

One man would carry a backpack loaded with grenades and Claymore mines. On the way out after the raid, it was his job to keep any pursuers off their backs. A trip wire made of fishing string attached to a grenade made for an effective booby trap. The hand-triggered Claymores, their most lethal anti-personal weapon, was to be used as a last resort, and when and if they were about to be caught or overrun.

Three other men would be armed with the newest models of the M79 rifle mounted grenade launchers. Every man would carry a knife of his own preference, but it was usually a Ka-bar. They were also armed with frag grenades and M16 rifles equipped with darkness penetrating Starlight scope. One machete per squad would be used by whoever's turn it was on the point. The two Americans completed the nine man squads.

That night, the three National Guard trucks were loaded with enough food and water to last them a week.

The final meeting of the Americans dealt with a major problem, the lack of current and reliable intelligence. A week prior to their meeting, a surveillance plane out of Puerto Rico photographed what appeared to be a large Sandinista camp in the central mountains. Days later, a Nicaraguan jet, flying at a much lowered altitude, reported seeing a similar looking camp, but twenty miles from its originally reported location.

"Two sightings," said Abner, "which could mean two different camps, or one camp with someone in charge who's smart enough not to stay camped too long in one place."

"Why," said the usually optimistic Poochie, "do I suddenly feel like we could be operating while blind in one eye and unable see out the other."

Several beers later, with no solution readily at hand, and unable to ask for another surveillance flight lest it give their unauthorized operation away, they did the logical thing that intelligent fighting men do in these situations. They flipped a coin. It came up heads. The Nicaraguan pilot's report was what they would bet the farm on...and possibly, a lot of lives.

Before they called the meeting to an end, each member of the Alpha team added one other small, but important item to their arsenal...a whistle.

During the seven hour drive to where they would leave the trucks and continue on foot, they were waved through two checkpoints manned by army troops. In each instance, because the trucks were marked *NATIONAL GUARD*, they were waved through without even being forced to stop. The cautious regular army troops had no wish to interfere with or get on the wrong side of the brutal and dreaded National Guard.

After pulling the trucks off the road and out of sight, it required less than ten minutes to camouflage the trucks and start moving to the south, the direction in which they hoped to find the Sandinista camp. If the surveillance information was close to being correct, the camp was fourteen to fifteen miles away, and at the base of the Cordillera Isabella Mountains.

The first hour of the march was slow going due to the thick foliage, and on several occasions, the need to skirt around small farms that looked to be uninhabited, but out of caution still had to be avoided. Shortly after they had circled around the last farm house, the landscape gradually changed. They were now moving through a lightly wooded terrain crisscrossed with small to medium size streams. Both the streams flowing in the opposite direction they were moving, and the gradual increase in elevation, were indications they were moving in the direction of the foothills. That was good, but better still, they stumbled upon a well-worn path filled with hoof marks made by either horses or mules. It was common knowledge that the Sandinistas often relied on horses or mules to transport men and supplies. In a terrain unsuitable to mechanized transportation other than a dirt bike, the rebels had no choice but to use animals or people to keep their soldiers supplied.

Abner and the other squad leaders agreed that the path would probably lead them to the Sandinista camp…if it hadn't been moved after the fly-over by the Nicaraguan jet.

Four hours later, as the sun began peeking over the nearby mountains, the scouts who had been out in front of the three squads returned and reported they were within a half mile of their objective. They also reported that they had found the rebel camp and that it was larger than anyone had anticipated, with as many as two-hundred Sandinistas spread out over at least a quarter of a mile.

Learning this, Abner called the squad leaders together, and went over some changes to the plan they had formulated the previous day.

"We can't follow the original plan to simply charge them and create as much damage as possible. Their camp is too spread out, and if we go charging in we're liable to get our asses surrounded and end up like Custer."

To his left, Abner could hear Willie grunt, followed by his saying, "Better to be an Indian."

"Agreed," said Abner, as he began to use his knife in the dirt to sketch out his revised plan. "I want our squads to tuck in tight a few hundred yards across from the center of their camp. Then we hit them hard with everything we've got, but for no more than five minutes."

Ron didn't have to hear or see anything more to recognize the rest of Abner's plan. It was a 'leap frog strategy' designed to lure an attacking enemy into an ambush, and in Viet Nam, the same plan had worked well. He remembered 'how well' because he and the Manchus had been on the receiving end of a VC ambush. Also, he knew that five minutes was enough time to do significant damage to the rebels, but probably not enough time for them to mount an organized counter-attack.

"Like hell," said Poochie, "we play hit 'em hard and then we run until we catch them."

CHAPTER 10

The plan came off without a hitch. From a distance of over three-hundred yards, the three squads began pouring thousands of rounds into the unsuspecting camp. When the designated five minutes had passed, as Abner had hoped, the center of the rebel camp began to fill up with reinforcements from the left and the right. Seeing this bunching up of the enemy, and believing they we're minutes away from mounting a counter attack, Abner used his whistle for the first time. Within seconds, the shrill sound of the whistle had the Blue squad and White squad up and moving to the rear. Abner observed the rebels were slower than expected to get organized, so he held the Triangle squad back just long enough to ensure the rebels knew where he and his men were and would take the bait. The delay also gave the other squads time to fully set the trap. No more than two minutes went by before he heard the sound of a whistle signaling him that the other squads were in place. It was time to for his squad to play the fox to the foxhounds.

"Move out," he shouted as bullets coming from the rebel camp began to pepper the Triangle squad's position.

Using the scope on his rifle, a final glance at the camp told Abner that the rebels, some of them undressed and shoeless, were indeed about to make their counter-attack.

"Looking good," shouted Willie, as both men turned and emptied their rifles in the direction of the camp before joining the rest of the squad in a dash to the rear.

Minutes later, they had passed between the two hidden Blue and White squads that had taken up positions on either side of the path. So well were they hidden, if it hadn't been for the muted sound of a whistle, neither Abner nor Willie would have known they were there.

The Triangle squad continued past the ambush sight for a hundred yards before stopping to reload their weapons and take cover. From there they would be able to fire at the oncoming rebels, and hopefully, direct the rebels' attention to them, and away from the squads lying in wait. The Triangle squad would be the bait and the Blue and White squads would be the two sides of the deadly trap, and the crossfire they would inflict on the Sandinistas.

The trap worked to perfection. Over twenty of the rebels were killed or wounded in the first few seconds of the ambush. In the next few seconds, a dozen more Sandinistas fell to the withering fire raining down on them. The sound of Abner's whistle signaled the Blue and White squads to break contact with the enemy, and the Triangle was now in place and ready to cover their retreat. The two squads instantly broke off contact with the rebels and went racing past the Triangle squad's location.

Like predators smelling blood, the Sandinistas went after what they thought was fleeing prey. Now reinforced by other rebels who had been slower at first to recover from the initial attack, the Sandinistas went after them. Phase two of the trap was now in effect. With their thinking clouded by anger and wanting revenge, the Sandinistas ran blindly into the gun sights of Abner's Triangle squad.

Caught in the second ambush in less than a few minutes, the Sandinista leaders who were still alive, and now more uncertain as to how many enemy they were facing, ordered their men to retreat. Only one man was not subject to that order.

Despite pleas to the contrary from their men, the Americans allowed the rebels to withdraw without further harm. The Americans knew it was now time to put as much distance as possible between themselves and the numerically superior rebels.

Before the Alpha team and their men began the long trek back to the trucks, they did a running head count of their dead or wounded. It amounted to five wounded, none seriously, and zero fatalities.

"Not too bad for a bunch of greenhorns," a smiling Lobo said to Abner.

"Not bad at all replied Abner, "even for…"

The one Sandinista who had not retreated with the others was Raul Garcia. Trained in Cuba a year earlier, he was a sniper, and had stayed behind to slow down or stop the enemy from pursuing his comrades. It was a time honored withdrawal tactic which went back to the bow and arrow era. It also required that the sniper have the courage to carry out his mission despite the inordinately high risk of being killed in the process. If he wasn't needed to cover the retreat, he had been trained to seek out any target of opportunity. Lobo, standing slightly over three-hundred yards away from where the sniper was hidden, became that target of opportunity.

The bullet nicked Abner on the lower part of his left arm before striking Lobo in the upper portion of his chest, driving him back several feet before hurling him to the ground. Abner's response was instantaneous. Ignoring his instinct to go to his wounded friend, he immediately went on the attack, and that meant disrupting or taking out the sniper before he was able to take down anyone else. Grabbing an M60 out of the hands of a soldier crouching feet away, he charged in the direction of the sniper. It wasn't a blind charge on his part. Based on the bullet's flight path, combined with the firm belief the sniper fire had come from no more than a few hundred yards to the rear of their position, he had already calculated the most likely line of the bullet's flight. That gave him the sniper's approximate position. With one glance in that direction, he picked out an area of heavy brush best suited to a sniper. Within seconds, he was moving in that direction while spraying the area with deadly rounds from the M60.

The Sandinista had chosen decent cover in a shallow depression hidden by bushes and a cluster of basketball-sized rocks. The rocks protected him from the bullets flying inches above his head, but not from his own fear. It was that fear, caused by the sight of a crazy giant coming at him with a deadly machine gun that broke his nerve. When the machine gun fire shifted momentarily to his left, he sprang to his feet and began running. He had covered less than thirty feet before his upper body was ripped apart by the 7.62 caliber shells. Thrown forward by the impact of the M60's large caliber bullets, he was dead before his face struck the ground.

Abner saw the sniper go down at the same time as the M60 went dry. Satisfied that the sniper was dead, he turned around and began jogging back to where Lobo had fallen. As he approached the group of men huddled around Lobo, he could see Willie and Poochie kneeling over the prostrate figure, desperately attempting to staunch the flow of bright red blood leaking from Lobo's chest. Abner had seen similar wounds in Viet Nam, and knew that rarely did anyone, even someone as strong and tough as Lobo, survive such a wound. The shaking of Willie's head and the look on Poochie's face told him the man who had fought at his side through so many battles, was dying.

The men of the Alpha team were shaken by the sight of their fallen comrade, but they also knew the chance of being seriously wounded or dying was a risk which all of them had accepted as part of their chosen profession. They also understood they had to get moving, that there wasn't time to spare for grieving, not with the strong possibility they were about to go from being the hunter to being the hunted.

After constructing a crude litter for Lobo from saplings used as poles stuck through the arms and legs of a jacket and pants, Abner gave the order to move out at double time.

With scouts positioned hundreds of yards to the front and rear, and their squad leader being carried by four men from the White squad, they moved out. Hours later, at the same place where they had first found the path which led them to the rebel camp, the two advance scouts were waiting for them.

"Dammit," said Abner to the soldier nearest to him, "get someone's ass out in front, because if the Sandinistas have somehow managed to get in front of us, we damn sure need to know about it."

He then turned his attention to the reason for the scout's dereliction of duty. They had captured a man and a loaded down pack horse. The man, who looked to be in his early thirties, was on his knees, with one of the scouts pressing the barrel of an M16 against his forehead.

Because he had been on the trail leading to the Sandinista camp, combined with his strong physical appearance, there was no doubt in anyone's mind the prisoner was anything but a rebel. The question of what to do with him was a horse of a different color. While Willie and Poochie were using the delay to tend to Lobo, Abner and Ron began questioning the prisoner.

It was decided that letting the men have him was one option. Leaving him alive but tied up to a tree was another. Taking him with them and turning him over to the National Guard was a third option. Had the two men, both hardened by the brutality of war, faced the same decision in Viet Nam, it would have been a no-brainer. One bullet, one problem solved...but they weren't in Viet Nam and they were no longer the same men they had been.

Abner's and Ron's decision was to take the prisoner with them. Although he didn't seem to be anything other than a common soldier, he could still be a valuable source of information.

When they approached the prisoner they were mildly surprised by his calm demeanor. They had expected him to be either shaking with fear, or filled with anger or defiance. He was neither of those things. When he looked at them, his face displayed no expression of animosity or fear. It was as if he was resolved to his fate and not in fear of it.

"Have you searched him?" Abner asked the man who continued to press his M16 to the prisoner's forehead.

"Yes," came back the reply, "there were no weapons."

"And the pack on the horse?"

"We found some food, clothes, blankets, and a few old newspapers, but not any weapons."

Abner and Ron were about to speak to the prisoner, but were interrupted by the sound of coughing coming from Lobo's litter. Ron, Abner, and the prisoner turned their face in that direction.

"I fear your friend is dying," said the prisoner in a soft voice which seemed compassionate rather than sarcastic.

"Yes," said a stoic Abner as he turned to look down at the prisoner.

"If you will permit me do so," said the man as he looked at Abner's face, "perhaps I can offer him some comfort."

"Not unless you're a doctor." replied Abner.

"I leave the care of a man's body to other hands. I am Father Rosales, and when I can, I care for the immortal souls of God's children."

As he was speaking, he reached into his shirt and pulled out a bronze cross hanging from a chain.

"You're a priest?" asked Ron, who as a lapsed Catholic hadn't been in a church for over a year.

"Yes, I am a priest."

Hearing these words, the soldier holding the rifle to the head of the prisoner, instantly stepped back in reverence and pointed the working end of the rifle at the sky.

Abner had to decide whether the prisoner was lying or speaking the truth. He was convinced, as much as could be, that the man kneeling before him was truthful.

After a momentary hesitation, he extended a helping hand to the prisoner. As the man rose to his feet, Abner noticed that he was fairly strong and had a heavily calloused hand. Neither of the features was something he associated with a priest.

"Please do what you can," said a now suspicious Abner.

"I will need something from my pack," said the prisoner.

A minute later, the priest removed a red blanket from underneath the canvas sheet covering the pack.

Folded as the blanket was, it was apparent to Abner and Ron it could easily conceal a weapon.

"So much for searching the blanket," said Ron.

"I noticed," replied Abner as he gave the scout holding the rifle a look of disapproval.

They both watched as the priest, carrying the blanket with the palms of his hands, made his way to where Lobo was lying. Moving slowly, he then placed the blanket on the ground and unfolded it to reveal a bible, a white stole, a communion cup, a linen cloth, and two small glass bottles. After removing the lid from one of the bottles and then touching the liquid in it to his fingertips, he gently touched the liquid to Lobo's eyes, ears, nostrils, hands and feet. When he was done, he began to make the sign of the cross.

At that moment, Lobo opened his eyes and slowly placed his hand on the priest's forearm. He then turned his face toward the priest and struggled to speak through the pink bubbling froth covering his lips. The words were so softly spoken only the priest, who had moved his face nearer to Lobo's, could hear them. Seconds later, Lobo's hand fell away from the priest's arm. He was gone.

"Eduardo Jorge Sanchez," said the priest, "go in peace with forgiveness of your sins by your God."

Hard hit by the death of his friend, Abner struggled to maintain his composure. Taking command, he knew getting the men he was responsible for to safety, was the solution to his problem.

"Slim," he said as he turned away from Lobo's body, "have your men place Lobo on top of the pack."

"On it," replied Slim.

"Poochie," said Abner, "you're the fastest man we've got, so you get the grand prize. As I remember it, there's a slight clearing a hundred yards back from where we just came. After we're gone, I want you to cover our asses. Set a claymore, and then wait there for half an hour, but not one minute longer. If any Sandinistas show up, you know what to do."

"Blow 'em to hell, and then get my feet moving," said Poochie.

"Like never before," replied Abner, "because when we get to the trucks, we can't risk waiting for you."

Two minutes later, the totally silent men, were on the move. Twenty minutes later they heard the muffled sound of an exploding claymore.

"Time to run," shouted Abner.

An hour later, when they reached the road, Abner brought the exhausted men to a halt. They were now only hundreds of yards from where they had left the trucks.

"Slim," said Abner, "take two men who can drive a truck with you. Check out the trucks and use your whistle if everything is a go."

Slim and the two men had barely crossed the road when a heavy breathing Poochie showed up at Abner's side. Abner noticed he was no longer carrying his rifle.

"Trouble?" asked Abner

"They got smarter this time," Poochie answered. "They had one man on point about a hundred yards in front of the main force. I let him pass and waited for the rest of them to show up. When they did, they were moving in a line with a gap of four or five yards between each man. The claymore took out a few of them in the front of the column, but missed the main force."

"They learned fast," said Abner.

He didn't waste time asking Poochie about the missing M16, or what happened to the single Sandinista. That could wait until later.

He did ask, "How far back are they?"

"Ten minutes, tops," said Poochie.

His response came at the same time as Slim began blowing on his whistle.

Abner responded by blowing on his own whistle. It was the signal telling Slim it was okay to bring on the trucks. A minute later, the wildly rocking trucks came crashing out of the heavy brush and onto the road.

Abner's order to mount up was ninety-nine percent wasted breaths. The army, led by those who had heard Poochie's report to Abner, filled the trucks within seconds.

Abner, who was the last man to climb into the back of the truck, made it a point to sit next to Father Rosales. There were still some question marks he wanted the priest to clear up. He began by offering the priest a canteen of water, followed by the offer of a cigarette. Both offers were silently accepted.

"Father, how is it that you know Lobo's real name," he asked, "it is something known by only few people outside of his close friends."

77

"When I was a boy living near Chinandega, we often worked side by side in the fields. Working in the fields is something I still do to help my congregation."

"I'm surprised that you recognized him after almost twenty years?"

"Would you ever forget the face of someone who protected you, someone who once took a dreadful beating for you?"

Abner had no response to that question, but it was something he knew Lobo would have done.

"Are you a Sandinista?" asked Abner, "because you seemed to be heading their way when you ran into us."

"A man can be a priest and a patriot," said Father Rosales, "and yes, I was on my way to the Sandinistas."

"Why?" asked Abner.

"It is too dangerous for them to come to me," replied the priest, "so I go to them."

"Do you understand that priest or patriot, when we get back to our camp, I'm obligated to hand you over to the National Guard?"

"If that is the will of God," said the priest, "then so be it."

"If it's not breaking the rules of the church," said Abner, "can you tell me what Lobo said to you just before he passed away?"

"It was a simple request, really. He asked to be buried in Chinandega. He also recognized me and asked me to conduct the service."

"And you agreed."

78

"It would be an honor, but as both his friend and commander, that decision is yours to make."

Abner had no problem with Lobo's burial request, nor did he believe his superiors would object to it. How to get around the problem of having a pro-Sandinista priest conduct the service was something he'd have to work on.

When they passed the checkpoints they had encountered the day before, the American's noticed them mysteriously deserted. A greater mystery was waiting for them an hour later.

The trucks were brought to a stop by the sight of an unmarked three-quarter ton truck parked on the road. Leaning casually against the hood of the truck was a lone figure. He had a cigar in one hand, a bottle of beer in the other, and an igloo cooler at his feet. He also had an M60 lying on the truck's hood. Abner, the only one among the Americans to have previously met him, had to laugh at what he was seeing.

Hearing Abner's laughter, Ron asked, "You know that party boy?"

"He's a leatherneck named Carlos, or at least that's the name he's using. He's also the guy who picked us up at the airport."

"You suppose he's got an extra beer or two?"

"You're telling me you'd be so uncouth as to drink beer while our men go thirsty?"

"You snooze you lose," replied a grinning Ron.

A minute later, after exiting the truck, the five remaining members of the Alpha team men, with beer in hand, were gathered around the front of the truck. A single beer bottle, unopened and unexplained, was placed on the hood of the truck. Carlos, who had noticed there were now five of the Alpha team and not six, needed no explanation.

"You crazy bastards have been busy," Carlos told them.

"Just a standard training exercise," replied Abner.

"Well," said Carlos, "while you were conducting your "training exercise," the National Guard moved in and took your camp."

"What happened to the men we left behind?" asked Abner.

"Trucked back to Managua under close guard," replied Carlos, "but not without putting a hurt on some of the National Guard troops."

"Could that have anything to do with a certain Captain Quintero?" asked Abner.

"Thanks to you guys, he's now Lieutenant Quintero," said Carlos, "and believe me, he wants a piece of your hide."

"I can handle him," replied Abner.

"Don't be too sure of that," replied Carlos. "He's also got about a hundred men with him, and they didn't come to exchange pleasantries."

"That bad?" said Ron.

"Bad enough that that all of you are personas non grata and I've got orders to take all of you to the airport and put your dumb asses on a plane back to the states," answered Carlos, "and no stopping by the camp to make nice with Quintero."

Abner then told Carlos about Father Rosales and the need to give Lobo the burial he had requested.

"I suppose you know that if Quintero gets his hands on a priest working with the rebels, regardless of the reasons, he'll be tortured and then killed."

"Which is why I've got a plan," said Abner.

Half an hour later, the trucks were hidden off the road and the men were gathered about the Americans.

"Listen up," Abner told them in his best Spanish, "because I've got bad news. While we were gone, National Guard soldiers under the command of Quintero, took control of our camp. As you might expect, he is not happy with us Americans. This means this must be the last time we will be together."

Abner then paused long enough to give what he said time to sink in.

"What I now ask of you, is that if and when you can, pass along what you have learned from us to others. Make us proud. Be their instructors. Make them into the fine soldiers you have become."

With the situation explained to them, the Nicaraguans readily agreed to Abner's plan. They would remain where they were for at least twenty-four hours before returning to camp.

As the truck driven by Carlos, and carrying the Alpha team and Father Rosales pulled away, the Nicaraguans were raising their rifles above their heads and yelling Manchu, over and over again.

Three hours later, they reached the darkened outskirts of Chinandega. It was Father Rosales who pointed out the home of Petrona Lau.

"You know her?

"When I was young, I was a thief and worse. It was Senora Lau who saw the good in me, and because of her unshakable faith in me, and God's forgiveness, that I entered the priesthood."

An hour later, it was Petrona Lau who promised the men of the Alpha team that their fallen comrade's grave site would be forever cared for in a way as if a member of her family. It was Father Rosales who presided over the ceremony. After the ceremony ended, he was freed to do as he wished.

None of the Lau family ever learned who left behind the envelope containing a thousand dollars of American money, along with a note asking that the headstone of Eduardo "Lobo" Sanchez be engraved with the word *MANCHU*.

CHAPTER 11

Chinandega, Nicaragua   **1981**

Although I had yet to reach my seventh birthday and Salvador was barely ten, even at that age we had a strong interest in what my father and his friends discussed during their weekly game of Desmoche which was held at our house in Chinandega. It was an interest my father always encouraged as long as we stayed out of the way and did nothing to distract our guests. Because of this, during their discussions, my brother and I would sit silently outside by an open window on the veranda, unseen and unheard, but able to hear everything being said. Years have gone by since then, but in my mind I can still hear the shuffling of the cards, the sweet smell of the coffee, and the pungent aroma of their cigars, all of it carried to me on the breeze created by the house's cross-ventilation.

But most of all, I remember the three men, and the passionate love they felt for the games of Desmoche, cock fighting, and their families. Being as young as I was, when it came to my father's priority, I was never sure of the exact order, but I do remember hearing my mother playfully accusing him of 'spending more time with the roosters than he did with his children.' It was shortly after that magical time I would learn that my father and his friends had a fourth passion, their country. It was a truth I would learn when the ideal world my parents had created suddenly fell apart.

Of my father's friends, Juan Campos de Leon

was easily my favorite. It was partially because he always came to the house with a small gift for myself and my brothers, and partially because he always spoke to me as if I were years older. He had a degree in law from the Universidad Nacional Autonoma de Nicaragua, but never practiced that profession, preferring to teach at the local Catholic high school. Born into a wealthy family with extensive cattle holdings in the area around Chinandega, he seemed to have little concern for money or the trappings of wealth. Tall and thin with white hair and a soft but commanding voice, I often wondered if he owned more than one suit.

Contrary to the social position of his parents and family, in previous years, he had been an ardent and sometimes open supporter of the Sandinistas. That was before they came to power, and before he understand how meaningless were the promises the Sandinistas had made to redistribute the land and create a better life for the common people. Forced out of his job at the school because of his liberal teachings, he had attempted to defend people arrested by the communist controlled police. That's when he learned that under the new system of justice, there was no adequate defense, and that all those accused, regardless of the circumstances, were automatically guilty. Warned by friends that he might be imprisoned because of his often outspoken views, he had sent his family to live in Honduras.

Arturo Reyes, a boyhood friend of my father's, not as well educated as Senor Campos, but not less intelligent, he was a farmer at heart who preferred working with his hands. It was those same calloused hands that could repair a tractor in the morning and lovingly play the strings of a guitar in the evening. Quiet and well- muscled with long arms and stout legs as were many Nicaraguans with mixed Indian and Spanish blood, to me, he represented the spirit of the peasantry. He was a simple man content with his life as a farmer and the pleasures he derived from family and friends.

Like Senor Campos, Ricardo Benevidez was also wealthy, and like many of the families in Nicaragua, his family had been split apart by the civil war which had gripped the country for over a decade. A cattle rancher who also raised fighting roosters as a hobby, he survived the last days of the Somoza's rule despite having a son who had been killed while fighting on the side of the Sandinistas. Because Ricardo now believed the loss of his son was for a false cause, and because a second son who had once considered joining the Sandinistas, was now, with his father's approval, across the border separating Nicaragua and Honduras...and a contra soldier, he was at now risk of being imprisoned by the Sandinistas. It was Senor Benevidez, along with Senor de Leon, who was now encouraging his friends to take themselves and their families out of the country.

"I urge all of you to reconsider any thought of staying here," Benevidez told them. "What the Sandinistas have done and will do is a repeat of what Castro did in Cuba after Batista was run out of that country. Castro, in order to silence any opposition to the communist government he planned to set up, had most of the country's intellectuals and professionals either shot or put in prison. The same thing will happen in Nicaragua after the Communists gain total control. There will be no law except their law. No true justice. And anyone even suspected of an act or belief not in line with the party line will be punished."

"You're telling us to leave our homes, leave everything behind?" questioned Geraldo's father. "I don't think moving to another country is acceptable."

Benevidez replied, "Yes, my advice is for you and your family to leave Nicaragua knowing that in all likelihood none of you will be able to return. The United States would take you, if you ask for political asylum for you and your family."

"I'll have to take some time to think about it."

Campos, who had been thoughtfully listening to the exchange, interjected in a voice reminiscent of his role as a teacher.

"I suggest you reach a decision as soon as possible. The block committees established by the Sandinistas are becoming increasingly powerful in their roles as spies and informers. They, like so many people given power, have resorted to lies and innuendoes to see that people in high places are brought low. Because you were a successful businessman under Somoza's regime and often outspoken about the people's rights and freedom, you are a likely target for the block committees. They would like nothing more than to see you and your family labeled political insurgents and taken to Managua's El Chipote prison. I have heard of, but not seen, the horrors prisoners are subjected to in El Chipote. Although there are only forty or fifty reported executions, thousands of others are purported to have been subjected to various forms of torture, including sleep deprivation and starvation."

A man of few words, compared to his companions, what I remember Senor Reyes saying that day was, "I might send my wife and children to Honduras or even the United States. But for myself, I will remain here, where I was born. If that means death or imprisonment, so be it."

Little did I know that a week later, the lives of myself and my family would so drastically change and that this would be the last meeting between my father and his friends.

CHAPTER 12

Chinandega, Nicaragua   1984

They came minutes after the rising sun, beyond the surrounding hills, began to cast long shadows over our home. They came, a dozen or more, riding in large trucks. They came armed with weapons and wearing the uniforms of the Sandinistas.

Perhaps it was the sound of the trucks breaking to a stop that woke me, or perhaps the sound of their heavy boots thudding against the hard ground. What I know for sure is that their arrival filled me with a terrible sense of dread, both for myself and my family.

I had heard of such raids by the soldiers of the newly formed government. Soldiers who came at night or in the early morning and took away anyone they deemed to be an enemy of the government. Many of those taken were never heard from again. Anyone seeking their whereabouts was warned by the authorities that if they were foolish enough to persist in their search they might suffer the same fate. The soldiers knew little of mercy. Many of them had lost family and friends in the fight to overcome the Somoza government. They were hardened to the killing and cruelty that a civil war brings to both sides of the conflict. They came to arrest people thought to oppose the new government. Only those people who resisted were not taken by the soldiers. For those people who resisted, there would be no prison and no tomorrow, only the eternal escape brought about by their deaths.

Too frightened to move from my bed, I heard the sound of the men crashing through our front door. A moment later a man carrying a weapon was standing in the door to my bedroom. Beyond him I could see several soldiers moving toward the other bedrooms where my parents and brother and sister slept.

As a soldier dragged me from my bed and took me outside to the veranda, I could hear men's voices shouting out orders, followed by what sounded like a struggle. Shortly after that, the other soldiers pushed my parents, Salvador and a sobbing Yahel out of the house. Through my own tears, I saw my father with blood running down his face from his forehead, and my mother clinging to his arm in a futile effort to pull him away from his captors.

One of the soldiers jerked my mother away from my father, pushed her roughly onto one of our wicker benches, and then turned his attention to myself and Salvador. We all stood shaking and silent as the men led my father toward the waiting truck. Not being able to stand silently any longer, I shouted at them, "Why are you taking my father?"

The soldier who had dragged me from my bedroom, stepped back into the veranda, and bent over until he was looking into my eyes from only a few inches away. Putting a hand on my shoulder he gave an answer to my question. By the tone of his voice and the expression on his face, I could not tell if he spoke out of kindness or cruelty.

"Your father has been judged to be an enemy of the revolution," he said, "and I believe it will be a long time before you see him again."

"Can we visit him?" asked Maritza after finally finding her voice.

The soldier could see how upset the family was, and although he was bound by duty to enforce the often merciless orders of the revolutionary leaders, he was not entirely void of a sense of compassion

"You will be allowed one visit each month," he told, "and only on a Saturday or a Sunday. You should make your first visit this weekend."

"Why?" questioned Maritza.

"There's is only enough food for the guards, but nothing for the prisoners. The prisoner's food has to be supplied by their families or friends, otherwise they face starvation. You will be allowed to bring 50 kilos of food every month. Bring him fruit, nuts, vegetables which require little or no cooking, and food such as flour, sugar, coffee, rice and beans. On your first visit, bring a large pot along with wooden cooking utensils. Metal utensils will be considered weapons and confiscated by the guards."

"Is there any other way I can help my husband?"

"Even if he doesn't smoke them, take him cigarettes and cigars he can use to trade for other things he will need."

"Thank you for the information, senor," said Maritza, "I will do as you suggest."

"I have one more suggestion for you," he said. "When you visit your husband, you will see things a woman should never see. It will be wise for you to control your emotions at the sights these things."

The following Saturday, Maritza appeared at the prison. As she had been warned, what she found was horrible. The smell of urine and feces, combined with the smell of thousands of unwashed bodies, was thick in the air, causing her hold her hand over her mouth to keep from gagging. The prison, designed to hold about 2,500 occupants, now held over 8,000. Many of the prisoners were forced to live outdoors with no protection from the sun, heat, or mud that resulted from frequent rain storms. The visit began with the guards thoroughly inspecting everything she carried with her. With inspections completed, the assembled visitors were told by a guard there would be a fifteen minute delay until they could proceed through the prison grounds.

Minutes later, the distinct sound of a volley of rifles reached the ears of those waiting. The sound of the shots almost brought tears to Maritza's eyes. She had heard rumors of executions being carried out in the prison, and now she dreaded the thought that her husband might be one of those victims.

After the brief delay, the guard led the group of visitors along the edge of an open air plaza. To her left, Maritza saw three bloody posts embedded in the ground. Next to the foot of each post, she saw a pool of bright red blood that brought the taste of bile to her throat. After passing through several gated enclosures, they reached a barren and sun soaked area that contained rows of benches, but no tables or chairs. At the sound of a whistle, the gates on the far side of the enclosure were opened, and prisoners, as many as fifty, entered the area,

Geraldo was one of the first prisoners through the gate, but in his stripped prison uniform, she struggled to find him among the other prisoners. He spotted Maritza immediately and waved to her. To her relief, he smiled and began walking toward her with the same air of confidence he always displayed.

"How are the children?" were the first words he spoke.

"They've gotten over their fright," she replied, "but they miss you terribly."

"Good, good, and how are you, my love?"

"My only concern is for you and how long you must stay in this horrible place."

"From what the other prisoners tell me, it could be a year, even two, before I am released."

He did not mention that for some more unfortunate prisoners who had no support from the outside, there was no release but one.

At the end of the one hour visitation period, Maritza embraced her husband and made her way out of the prison to begin the journey back to Chinandega.

It was a journey she would repeat monthly, not for a year or even two, but for almost four years.

CHAPTER 13

Chinandega, Nicaragua   1987

Returning home after another monthly visit to her husband, Maritza found Senors Reyes, Benevidez, and Campos waiting for her. It was the first time since Gerardo had been taken away that all three men had paid her a visit at the same time. Because of this she felt that they must have something important to discuss with her.

"Have you heard anything about when Gerardo might be released?" asked Senor Benevidez.

"He told me that there is little chance of his being released this year, but thinks it will happen next year," replied Maritza, "but I have learned that nothing is certain when it comes to what the Sandinistas will do."

"We can pray that the day of his return will come soon," said Senor Reyes.

"Yes," said Maritza, "we can pray, but I suspect something other than prayer has brought you to my home."

It was Senor Campos who responded to her words.

"The Sandinistas are having a hard time with the contras. Many of Samosa's soldiers have been killed or wounded, and others, tired of the killing of their own countrymen, have simply gone home. Also, and it's a growing movement, some soldiers have deserted the army and gone over to the side of the contras. Because of the losses, the Sandinistas has begun to recruit and conscript boys as young as fourteen. I don't think I have to remind you that Salvador is fast approaching that age."

"That is true," Maritza replied as she turned her face to look at her oldest son. Gazing at him, Maritza suddenly realized he was no longer a boy, but a young man who was physically mature and tall for his age. Her heart sank with the thought that he could be forced into the army and lost to her.

"I don't want to see any of my sons taken by the army," she said, "and there's nothing I won't do to prevent it."

"That's why we are here," Benevidez said. "We believe that to keep Salvador out of the clutches of the army, he must get out of the country. With money spent in the proper places, it should not be difficult to get him across the Honduran border and out of the reach of the Sandinistas. That would also hold true for you, Moises, and Yahel if you decide to go with him.

"I understand you have relatives in Teguche," said Senor Benevidez.

Yes, my sister Maria and her family. She would willingly take in my Salvador, but I will never abandon my home unless my husband is with me," she said.

"And while I understand the need for Salvador to leave immediately, and although it might put them at some risk, I could not bear to be away from Moises and Yahel, not even for a few months."

"Actually," said Senor Benevidez, "there is a risk involved if you stay, but it may also be a wise thing to

94

do. Sandinistas spies may never take notice of Salvador's absence, but if your entire family suddenly disappears, there is little doubt that it would be quickly brought to the attention of the authorities."

"And that might mean trouble for your husband," added Senor Reyes.

"Then," said Maritza, "we should prepare for what we have to do."

During the next three days, Maritza, with the help of Gerardo's three good friends, made arrangements for Salvador's escape to Honduras. On the fourth day, with Yahel and Moises standing by their side, Maritza and her mother watched as Senor Reyes picked up the tearful Salvador and drove him away. It would be a full year before they would see him again.

A month later, two Sandinista with a dog on a leash, came to the house looking for Salvador. Although they accepted her story that he had run away weeks before, by the look of doubt on their faces, Maritza suspected they knew otherwise.

That night, Maritza fell into a fitful sleep, but not before wrapping her remaining children in her arms, and then saying a prayer to Jesus, asking him to protect Salvador. It became ritual she would repeat each night until her husband was released from prison. That day came almost one year later.

When Gerardo walked out of the prison and into the waiting arms of his wife and children, he tried to appear his old confident and strong willed self. But the time he had spent in prison had changed him both physically and mentally. His body, once strong and athletic, had been reduced to skin and bones by the forced labor demanded by the guards. His teeth, once gleaming white, were now brown and decayed. He had once stood taller and straighter than most men, but now he was bent at the waist, and with a posture usually found in much older men.

Maritza's heart went out to him. She understood how important his appearance had been to him before his imprisonment four years earlier, and that his present appearance had to be embarrassing to him. She now felt compelled to restore that pride, to rebuild and reclaim him. She would somehow restore him to the life he once had, a life filled with the love and friendship of family and friends. She wanted him to have a life which made each coming day something to be looked forward to by her husband and the entire family. But first, her family must leave Nicaragua and find another home in another country, and that meant going to America. It was a thought which filled her mind with equal amounts of hope and depredation.

By noon of the following day, Geraldo, who had been planning his family's escape during his four year imprisonment, laid out the plan to his family and his most trusted friends, Senors Reyes, Benevidez, and Campos.

"My wife, bless her soul, has spent the last four years accruing every bit of money she was could. That money, along with the money left over from her inheritance, should be enough to make our way to the United States, but it leaves us with the question of what to do with our house, our trading company, and the

96

store. If I were to try to sell them now, it would be sure to draw unwanted attention to us. It is my hope that Juan will accept the deed to my home. I want Arturo to be the new owner of the trading company. Ricardo, you will get the store, but I regret to tell you that it does not include Maritza. Her, I will keep."

Gerardo's humorous comment, followed by the laughter of everyone in the room, told Maritza that her husband's recovery from his four year ordeal in prison, was coming even sooner than she had dared to hope.

"I give you these things," she heard her husband say as she fought back her tears, "out of gratitude for the care and love you have given to my family while I was away."

"I will certainly accept your offer," said Arturo, "and when the time is right, I will sell the house and forward the money to you."

Juan and Ricardo agreed to do the same thing with the store and the trading post. None of the three men had the heart to tell him that because of the nation-wide rationing of almost every commodity, none of what he owned was worth more than the lumber and nails holding them up.

"Now that that problem is out of the way, I believe it's time to discuss an escape plan," said Gerardo. "I will begin by asking Juan to do as he did for Salvador and arrange to get us out of Nicaragua and into Honduras."

"That I may no longer be able to do," responded Juan, "Of course I will try, but all but one of my friends who helped me in such manners have been arrested, killed, or found their own way out of the country."

Before Gerardo could reply, Arturo said, "I don't want you to use the money Maritza has saved. You may need all of that money to get to the United States. I will gladly supply whatever money needed to get your family to Honduras."

It was an offer echoed by the other men in the room.

"But no man could have better friends," was all that Gerardo could say after declining the offers.

"And I believe those same friends would now like to hear the details of the plan you have to get your family to safety." said Maritza, "as would your trusting wife and children."

"Certainly," said Gerardo, "and please, I want all of you to feel free to offer any advice or correct me if I have left out anything important."

"I can hardly wait for such an opportunity," said a grinning Juan.

Gerardo had to wait for the second sounds of laughter to die down before continuing.

"My plan begins by keeping our preparations and departure unnoticed by any of the block community's spies. In prison, I thought about leaving in the middle of the night, but if we did that and were seen by the wrong people, our escape might be over before it began. I believe it will be better to leave here in the early part of the day, preferably on Sunday when everyone is out on the streets after church. Hopefully, this will enable us to blend in with the traffic going north."

"And when we get to the border?" asked Maritza.

"When we get to the border," answered Gerardo, "we will claim that we're going to the wedding of your niece in Teguche. To substantiate this story, we will carry with us a wedding invitation, our best clothes, and your wedding dress which your only niece insists she be married in."

"I like your idea about the wedding dress," said Maritza, "but I think we should also take several brightly wrapped wedding gifts with us. Having presents in the car would support our story that we're going to Honduras to attend a wedding."

"I believe your wife's suggestion is an excellent one," said Arturo, "but words and presents alone may not carry the day. I also suggest that you have several bottles of expensive champagne lying in plain sight. When the car is searched, and it will be searched, the guards will be less likely to be suspicious of you if their attention is focused on the bottles of champagne."

On the following Sunday, the Baranovicht family attended church as usual, and after the service was over, piled into their five year old Volkswagen van laden with wedding gifts. Without looking back or crying, they drove north to what they had prayed would be a new and better life.

When they reached the border at El Guasaule they fell in line behind a dozen or more cars and trucks. In front of them, they could see the passengers in the cars whose turn it was to be inspected, being forced to stand outside of the cars while they and their vehicle were searched by soldiers. To the relief of the Baranovichts, only one car was detained. That car, carrying four young men, was ordered to move to the right where the four men were pulled from the car and rudely escorted to a nearby building. The sight of the one story building which had only a single door and no windows, so reminded him of a similar building where his prison guards took 'special prisoners,' that it sent chills through Gerardo.

"May God have mercy on those poor men," he said to Maritza.

She was about to repeat his words but the sight of a soldier staring at them caused her to audibly suck in her breath.

"Stay calm," whispered Gerardo, who had also noticed the soldier looking right at them. "That stare he's giving us is done to test us, to see if we become overly nervous, as if we had something to hide."

"I know that face," Maritza whispered back. "He's the same man who was in charge of the soldiers who took you away to prison."

Gerardo then studied the man's face and quickly realized she was correct. It was the same man…and he was now walking toward them with his eyes fixed in their direction. Seconds later, after he had walked past the cars in front of them, he was standing by Maritza's open window.

"Good afternoon," he told her. "I am Captain Vargas, and may I ask what business you have in Honduras?"

"We plan to attend my niece's wedding next Sunday in Tegucigalpa," replied Maritza, "and to visit with relatives we haven't seen in years."

"That is a good thing to do," replied Captain Vargas. "Nothing is as important as family."

He then looked at the two children in the back seat.

"Your children are fine looking young people, the kind I'm sure any mother and father can be proud of."

"Thank you for such kind words," replied Maritza, "and we are proud of them."

"Excellent," he replied, "but now I must ask you to follow me."

For a brief moment Gerardo thought about slamming the car into gear and trying to break through the check point, but with so many armed soldiers present, he had no choice but to comply.

Hardly able to breathe, Gerardo and Maritza watched as Vargas then turned and walked around the front of the van, looked back at them, and then, with a slow wave of his hand, indicated he should be followed…but then he did the unexpected. He began leading them, not to the building on the right where the four men had been taken, but to the left and toward the check point's last gate.

When the front of the van was only a few feet from the gate blocking their way, Vargas held out his hand to signal that he wanted the van to stop there. Moments later, he had his hand on the window frame where Gerardo was sitting."

"Senor Baranovicht, before you leave Nicaragua, I want you to know that I regret any injustice that I may have contributed to, and I wish you and your family all the good fortune you deserve," he said in a sincere voice, "and perhaps, if God permits it, someday my family will be fortunate enough to receive an invitation to a wedding in Honduras, or somewhere even better."

Without waiting for a response, Vargas then turned and nodded to the soldiers manning the gate. He did not tell them that had it not been for his elderly parents who were too frail to travel, he would have left Nicaragua years before.

After leaving the Nicaraguan checkpoint, the van reached the Honduran checkpoint, and stopped in line behind other cars and trucks waiting to get into Honduras. Maritza used that waiting time to speak with her husband.

"Without looking at our papers, or us telling him our name, that man knew who we were," she told him, "and I'm certain he knows we weren't leaving Nicaragua to go to a wedding."

"I know," replied Gerardo. "I've been wondering if he may have been the one remaining contact Juan mentioned."

"It's possible," replied Maritza, "but I prefer to believe he's simply a good man who was somehow trapped in a horrible job, and who felt he owed us because of his part in your imprisonment."

"I'd like to think that's true," said Gerardo, "that some decency and humanity survived in even the cruelest of times."

"It's interesting that he was once with the National Guard, but now he's with the Sandinista ," said Gerardo, "maybe he's a spy for the contras."

"Whatever or whoever ever he is," replied Maritza, "I think he risked more than we may ever know to help us."

Other than having the bottles of champagne confiscated without being given a reason, they passed through the Honduran checkpoint without any trouble. Several hundred miles from where they were, a second group of people trying to cross into Honduras from Nicaragua were traveling a far more treacherous road.

CHAPTER 14

They were worn out, lost, hungry, and the heat and humidity could not have been any more oppressive, but still the three young people who had left San Sabastion de Yali days before, pushed on in the direction of the Rio Coco. It is what desperate people fearing for their lives will do. And these people, all of them less than twenty years old, did not want to die. Their singular goal, their one shared dream, was to get out of Nicaragua and make their way to the United States of America.

There could have been many more people in the group, but the man who had been paid to guide them across the Nicaraguan-Honduran border had insisted he wouldn't act as a guide for more than three people, claiming that more than that would slow them down and make them too easy for government patrols to detect. He was the same man who deserted them a day earlier, taking with him the money their grandparents had paid him, along with most of their food. Making their difficulties even worse, hours later, when they were spotted by a government patrol, they barely escaped being captured, and almost at the cost of losing the back pack containing the compass and the box of matches. Now they were facing even longer odds against reaching the United States.

Perhaps it was because of their youth, or perhaps their unalterable faith in a benevolent God, but nothing that had happened to them had in any way changed their minds about reaching their goal. Poor, and having lost their parents at an early age, they'd been toughened from childhood by the hours of back breaking work in the cane fields. Losing their guide, and most of their money, was looked upon as just another obstacle to be met and overcome. Courage and tenacity was a commodity they would never be short of.

The girl was seventeen and her name was Solidad Louisa Garza. Her brother Pepe was thirteen. Carolina was her fourteen year old sister. All three were tired and hungry as they pushed through the heavy scrub brush that pulled at their light clothing and tore at their skin. It had been that way for hours, ever since their encounter with the patrol. Now, with only minutes of daylight left, they were searching for a place to spend the night. Finding a small clearing beneath a stand of wild banana trees surrounded by tall grass, they collapsed on the ground for several minutes before finding the strength to begin setting up the camp. That began by stringing a light rope between two trees and hanging a thin plastic drop cloth over it. This created a triangular shaped tent which would keep the night time humidity off them, and dry in the event of rain. The erecting of the tent was followed by a meal of crackers, cheese, and green bananas taken from overhead. A Sterno can gave out just enough fire to boil water to make a single cup of coffee in their one remaining tin cup.

After they finished eating and blowing out the fire, they crawled into the tent, and using their backpacks for pillows, prepared to go to sleep. Minutes later, the last of the sunlight was replaced with a

moonless night sky, casting the area into absolute
darkness.

"Are we lost?" asked Carolina as she tapped her
brother on the arm.

"No," replied Pepe, "we have the map and we're
still moving north."

Solidad, no less worried than her sister, was
listening to them but said nothing. She knew that unless
you know where you're starting from, a map is just a
piece of paper, and she had only a questionable idea of
where they were, or how far it was to the river.

"Both of you need to go to sleep," she told them.

Within minutes both of them were soundly
asleep. She was able to stay awake just long enough to
whisper a prayer to Saint Christopher.

Thanks to the sound of someone or something
moving outside of the tent, Solidad was awakened at
daybreak. Her initial thought was that either Pepe or
Carolina might have made the sound, but a glance to
her right showed her that both of them were still
sleeping. She continued to lay motionless for several
moments while trying to understand what caused the
noise, but neither heard nor saw anything more.
Thinking it might be an animal, or even a snake, she
began searching for anything which would serve as a
weapon. The only thing her slowly moving hand found
was one of Pepe's sandals. With the sandal gripped
tightly in her hand, she crawled out of the tent, ready to
bravely defend herself and her brother and sister from
an unknown threat. The threat that greeted her eyes
came in the form of a single individual sitting cross-

legged on the ground about fifteen feet away from the tent.

"Good morning," he told her in a soft voice, "I'm Julio, and I hope you slept well."

Caught totally off guard, Solidad's voice failed her, but her eyes did not. The figure sitting across from her appeared to be about twenty years old, of medium build, was dressed in the simple clothes of a peasant, and as far as she could tell with only a glance, was unarmed. She also noticed that he had a pleasant face made more so by a broad lipped smile.

"I did," she replied in a voice she hoped matched his in its calmness.

Nothing more was said for a few moments, but it was long enough for Solidad to wish she had a more favorable appearance. In contrast, Julio thought he was looking at one of the more naturally attractive girls he had ever encountered.

It was Solidad who broke the silence by asking, "How did you find us and what do you want?"

"I didn't find you," replied Julio, "Chico did."

It was an answer which caused her to quickly glance to her left and right, looking for a second man. Seeing this and wanting to ease her fear, Julio brought two fingers to his mouth and made a low whistling sound. Almost instantly, a huge dog burst from the tall grass behind him. After looking at Solidad with its large brown eyes, it proceeded to sit down next to the man calling himself Julio.

Solidad had been raised around dogs of many breeds and sizes, but she had never seen such an imposing animal. It was big, bigger than any dog she had ever seen. With its large head, short ears, and rounded face surrounded by long fur, it looked to be more bear than dog. Its fully curled tail and white and brown colored coat were the only solid clues that it was more dog than anything else. When the animal did fix his eyes on her, it took every ounce of determination she could muster not to shrink back in fear.

"What kind of dog, if it is a dog, is that?" she stammered.

"This," said Julio as he patted the animal on the head, "is Chico, and he's a Japanese Akita."

"Is it…?"

"Oh yes, he is very dangerous?" said Julio before she could finish her question, "especially when he meets strangers."

In an instant he wished he could take back his words. By the look of concern which came to her eyes, it was obvious she didn't understand the humor in his words. Attempting to reassure her in the only way he could think of that Chico wasn't a threat, he playfully ruffled the dog's neck.

The dog responded by licking his face before collapsing on the ground with its tongue out and its wagging tail slapping against the ground.

"As you can see," said Julio as he rubbed the dog's head, "he's a bad, bad boy."

Solidad was now convinced that the dog was unlikely to hurt her or anyone else, but she still wasn't sure the same could be said for the stranger sitting across from her.

"Why are you here?" she demanded to know.

His answer came in the form of a question.

"Is this the first time you and your friends have tried to get to Honduras?"

Now believing from his appearance and the presence of the friendly dog that Julio was not military, but probably from a local town, she saw no reason not to give him an honest answer.

"They are my brother and sister, and this is the first time for all of us."

"It's my second time," said Julio. "My brother and I got across the Rio Grande the first time, but the Border Patrol caught us the next day. After spending two months in a detention center, we were deported back to El Salvador."

He went on to tell her that months ago his brother had been killed because he refused to join one of the gangs who were beginning to flourish throughout the country.

"Is that why you and Chico left home?" she asked.

"It's why I left," he answered, "but I never met Chico until he showed up about three weeks ago. When he found me, he had a chewed through rope tied to his collar. I gave him some food and we've been together since then."

"What do you feed him?"

"He usually catches his own meal," replied Julio. "He eats rodents, worms, wild pigs, lizards, anything that's slower than he is. He shares them with me, and I share with him the birds I take down with my slingshot."

While she was listening to him, Solidad was gradually becoming more comfortable in his and the dog's presence. Because of what he had told her about his background and his previous attempt to get to the United States, she was now entertaining the thought that he might be of help to them…but would he? And because of what had happened with the guide, did she dare trust him? She decided trusting him involved less risk than trying to get to the United States without someone's help.

"I would like you to help us," she told him, "and I can pay you a small amount, but how do I know I can trust you not to rob us?"

Julio took a moment to consider her offer, and at the same time think of some way to gain her trust. He knew that without his assistance, the girl and her brother and sister had almost zero chance of reaching their destination. It was far more likely that they would end up dead. It was not a fate he would want any of them to suffer, especially the girl.

"I have money of my own," he answered, "but I would still like to join you."

Seeing that she still had a look of doubt in her eyes, he then stood up, turned his back to her, and pulled his shirt up to his shoulders.

"These were given to me after my brother and I tried to protect our neighbors from the gangs. I paid them back as best I could for killing him, but I can never go back."

Solidad's reaction to this was to place her hand over her mouth in an effort to smother a gasp of horror. She failed. The sight that greeted her eyes was so horrible, and spoke of such an unimaginable suffering, that the gasp came out as a cry. Long stripes of raised red flesh, some of them not completely healed over, covered his entire back. It was obvious that someone, someone with no conscience or a great deal of hate, must have used a whip to inflict such devastating wounds.

Solidad and Julio sealed their agreement to travel together with a handshake. Chico expressed his approval by getting between them and leaning against her leg.

By late in the evening of the following day, Julio had led them to within sight of the Rio Coco which separates Honduras from Nicaragua.

"We should cross the river in the morning," suggested Julio, "somewhere downriver where it's shallow enough to wade across."

"Shouldn't we do that now?" asked Solidad, "in case government troops find us on this side of the river."

"This may come as a surprise to you," Julio replied, "but the Sandinistas don't really care who gets out of the country, only who gets in. They won't come within miles of here because they're a lot more worried about running into gun carrying contra soldiers than they are with stopping people like us from getting into Honduras."

Minutes later, they had set up camp and Julio had a small fire going. When that was done, Julio extracted a hand sized plastic container from his bedroll. It was the type of container normally used to hold a bar of soap.

Seeing the container, Solidad hoped she could use the soap it contained to bath herself clean in the river. That hope was quickly turned to disappointment when Julio opened the container and displayed an assortment of fishing hooks and string.

"If anyone wants to go with me and Chico," he told them as he rose to his feet, "one of the world's greatest fisherman is about to go to the river and catch our dinner."

Carolina and Pepe were more than willing to accept his offer, but were held back when their sister told them, "You and Carolina need to stay here and guard the camp from thieves and wild animals."

As it turned out, Julio lived up to his bragging by catching enough fish to feed all of them, Chico included. Down river and out of Julio's sight, Solidad was able bath in the river using sand instead of soap. That night, everyone gorged on the fish which was cooked on sticks held over an open fire, with flat rocks from the riverbed serving as plates. After the last of the fish was eaten, the three invigorated siblings told Julio that it was the best meal they ever had.

It was a description with which a well fed Chico, if he could have talked, would have agreed.

While making their way through Honduras, they slept anywhere that provided even a minimum of protection from the elements, and even more importantly, out of sight of the Honduran police. But the police, and the possibility of being arrested and sent back to Nicaragua, was not the greatest threat they faced. That larger threat was the gangs who preyed on any outsiders they deemed to be too weak to defend themselves, or after being robbed, not be willing to risk reporting the attacks to the local police. Such assaults usually meant robbing them of everything they had, but in some cases, the gangs resorted to kidnapping, rape, and murder in addition to robbery.

Julio did his best to prepare Solidad and her siblings for an attack by these gangs. He insisted that all of them carry glass water bottles which, when a threat arose, could be broken and used as weapons. In addition to the slingshot, he also had a two-foot long three-quarter inch water pipe tucked into his bed roll. On two occasions when they were threatened by a gang, his preparations paid off. Just seeing the weapons and the snarling Chico proved to be enough to discourage two small gangs who decided that Julio and the others weren't the easy prey they were looking for.

It was after the second encounter with a gang that Julio realized the girls, being as young and attractive as they were, were probably what the gangs were after. At Julio's suggestion that Solidad and Carolina needed to change their appearance for the good of everyone, the girls cut off their waist length hair, and kept their faces smeared with dirt. Solidad also did her best to alter her naturally feminine walk to one which more closely resembled that of a man. By constantly wearing a serape, she also kept her more eye catching attributes hidden from the eyes of the public. Carolina, who had yet to lose her boyish shape, had no need to do either of these things.

By either walking or catching rides on trucks, they managed to travel through Honduras in eight days. Always moving north, but with no specific route they had to adhere to, on the ninth day they reached the small seaside town of Puerto Cortes on the Gulf of Honduras. Seeing that everyone was exhausted from their time on the road, Solidad suggested that they stay in the town for a day to rest.

That one day was to turn into a week after Julio learned he was the only one in the group who had ever seen an ocean, and more disturbing, he learned that none of them knew how to swim.

"Never?" he had asked them. "You never learned how to swim?"

The answer he received was silence followed by the shaking of three heads.

"Then we will stay here until you learn," he told them. "I don't want you to be like the people who couldn't swim and drowned trying to get across the Rio Grande."

If they had been asked, the four of them would have readily admitted that the next few days were the happiest days they had ever known.

After first buying swim suits from a second hand clothing store, they camped on the beach, cooked on a piece of flat iron fueled by driftwood, showered daily under an outdoor water faucet connected to a public bath, and spent hours playing and learning to swim in the water. For Julio, seeing Solidad in a bikini was a huge eye opener. Suddenly her legs were longer, her lips even redder, her eyes brighter, and her skin, when wet, glistened in the sunlight and glowed in the moonlight.

He had known from the first day they met that she was pretty, but never had he imagined that she, or maybe any girl, could look that spectacular. His feelings for her, which had been slowly becoming that of a brother or a cousin, now underwent a complete alteration. Uncertain how she would respond if she knew of his feelings, it was an alteration he tried to hide.

Carolina and Pepe loved the water and were quick to learn how to swim. By the third afternoon, they were swimming in water over their heads, riding the waves, and leaving Chico on the shore to bark out his concern for their safety. But as fast as they became accomplished in the water, they were no match for their sister. Her natural grace on land became magically magnified in the water. Now tanned all over, and with a supple body hardened by the journey, within days she had become a beautiful child of the sand and water, able to swim with speed and ease as she churned through the waves and the blue-green water.

About ninety yards from the beach was a coral reef which dropped down about twelve feet to the bottom on the near side of the shore and double that on the far side. Several times, a curious Solidad observed men in small boats dive down on the far side of the reef, and emerge holding a lobster, or a fish flopping on a spear. After watching the divers for the second time, she was confident that she could do what they did, and save money otherwise spent on food. With this in mind, she turned to Julio for help.

"If you can make a sling shot," she told him, "why can't you make a spear gun?"

"I could," he replied, "if I had the time and the materials, but I've got a better idea."

"Don't you always?" said a smiling Solidad who had come to enjoy teasing him.

Julio ignored her playful sarcasm and replied, "You wait here until I get back."

Solidad said nothing in reply as he began jogging off the beach until he was out of sight behind some of the town's buildings. He returned a half hour later carrying a spear gun, an inflated tire tube, one pair of goggles, and one of the net-like bags used to carry oranges.

"I don't see a boat," she teased.

"Boats are too expensive to rent," he replied, "so I settled for a spear gun, the goggles, and the inner tube."

Coming from a life where little money was used in favor of trading for what was needed, it had never occurred to her to rent anything. Concerned that Julio had spent too much money, money which they would need later on, she had to ask, "How much did those things cost us?"

Julio did not miss the fact that she had said 'us' for the first time. Always looking for an opportunity to tease her, he replied, "They cost *me* a dollar, and my promise to give the owner some of the catch if there was any."

"You're my hero," she told him before grabbing the inner tube out of his hands and running joyously into the water. Julio, who was left standing by himself and aware of nothing except how beautiful a picture she made as she ran, couldn't move as she stopped in knee deep water and turned to face him. For a long moment, she simply looked into his eyes, but neither moving nor speaking as several small waves gently broke around her legs. When she smiled at him, it was a small smile, the smile of a woman who knew his thoughts. It was a moment in time he would never forget.

After reaching the far side of the reef, they took turns diving for the lobsters and using the spear gun. They made a good team, with Solidad being better at catching lobsters, and Julio at spearing the fish. During the next few hours, they moved along the coral reef, marveling at the abundance of colorful life around it which including a green turtle and an inquisitive eel. Despite the distractions, they stuffed the orange bag with eight lobsters, and had twice that number of large fish dangling on a string tied to the inner tube. With more lobsters and fish than they could eat in a single meal, the now tired and happy couple decided it was time to return to the beach.

Halfway back to the beach, Julio stopped to retie the bag full of lobsters which had come loose from the inner tube. At one point, while he was retying the bag, their bodies touched when a wave pushed them together, making her acutely aware that he was...

Solidad responded by launching her body against his and planting a long and passionate kiss on his mouth. It was a kiss which took both their breaths away...and the birth of a heated romance that knew no boundaries.

She never told him that the loosening of the lobster bag wasn't an accident. He never told her that he had seen her untie the bag...or that he had seen the wave coming at them and could have easily avoided it.

CHAPTER 15

Despite the presence of a large number of soldiers on the streets of the bustling city, the Baranovichts had no problems when they reached Tegucigalpa. After picking up Salvador and then spending a night in a hotel, they were up early and drove to the Toncontín International Airport where they were able to purchase tickets to Mexico City with little attention paid to them. The same thing happened when they reached Mexico City and Maritza went to the Aeromexico ticket counter and requested tickets to the border city of Matamoras. In both instances, they did not attempt to purchase tickets which would take them directly to San Antonio, their final destination. They feared, that had they done so without being able to show the correct papers needed to go there, they would have been turned away. With only their birth certificates and no picture IDs, they decided to wait until they got to Matamoras...and hope their luck held for a little while longer.

After departing the plane in Matamoras, Gerardo used a pay phone to call Eastern Airlines and reserve five tickets to San Antonio. He hoped that by making the reservations over the phone, it would mean less time spent at the counter, and therefore less time for the busy ticket agents to question them.

With that plane not due to take off for several hours, they spent an hour eating lunch in a cafeteria. When they finished the meal, they moved to a row of chairs which gave them a clear view of the ticket counter. Twice while they were waiting, Gerardo walked by the counter, trying to determine how stringent the ticket agents were about checking passenger identification papers prior to issuing a ticket. His spirits dropped when he saw that all the passengers checking in had to show several forms of identification. This was bad news, but he also knew that he and Maritza had one important thing going for them, something most of the passengers lacked. Every member of his family spoke fairly good English, good enough for them to be mistaken as longtime residents of San Antonio.

Relying on their ability to speak English wasn't the best of gambles, but he knew it was the best one they had.

Gerardo spent part of the next hour explaining to his children what to do if things went wrong.

"Your mother and I will go to the counter to get our tickets. I want all of you to stay in your seats and keep your eyes on us. If things go as hoped, we will come back to our seats with the tickets, but if not, all of us may have to run out of the airport as fast as we can."

When the ticket agent asked for their identification papers, Gerardo turned to Maritza and held out his hand. Her response, which they had previously rehearsed, was to ask, "Don't you have them?"

"No," he replied, "I thought you did."

The agent was no fool, and their ploy, the same one he'd heard many times before, failed to deceive him.

"If you don't mind waiting," he told them as he picked up a telephone, "let me see if my manager can help you."

Gerardo immediately took Maritza by the shoulders, spun her around and shouted to his children, "Run."

The Baranovicht family, carrying their small bags, ran and kept running until they were well away from the airport. When they stopped to look for any pursuers, to the surprise and relief of all of them, there were none. What they failed to understand was that the airline employees, including the security personnel, had little reason to go after them. Preventing people from illegally boarding a flight out of the country meant that they had done their job. Actually catching those people was not in their job description…or worth the risk of getting hurt in the process.

Now faced with no chance of flying to the United States, Gerardo had to try the only option open to them. That option was to hire a dangerous and expensive coyote, those men took illegal immigrants across the Rio Grande for a hefty price, and if they had enough money, far into the interior.

"But, how do we find a coyote we can trust?" asked Maritza.

From his time in prison, Gerardo knew the answer, as did half the population of Matamoras.

"There's a large indoor market in the center of town. After we find a hotel, I'll go there and find a coyote. From what I heard in prison, they hang around bus stations and stores selling backpacks, looking for customers like us. What I don't know, is if we have enough money to pay them."

Later that day, after returning from the market, a dejected Gerardo had to tell his family he had found a coyote he felt they could trust, but that they had barely enough money to pay for two people, and that money had to be paid in advance.

Hearing this need for additional money, Maritza decided that it was the time to play a trump card, one she hadn't revealed to her husband. It was a phone call she had hoped wouldn't be needed.

"We've been in contact for years," she informed her husband, "ever since you were imprisoned. More than once she told me that if we ever needed money to help us get to Texas, she would be willing and able to help."

Two days after making the call to her sister, Maritza and her husband went to a Wells Fargo bank, and after showing what identification papers they had, left the bank with an envelope containing five thousand dollars stuffed in her purse. The next day, following orders from the coyote using the name Hector, they, along with more than a dozen other men, women, and two teenage girls, were crammed into the back of a box trunk. It was totally dark inside the truck, and only once during the following hours, was the truck stopped and the rear doors opened long enough to let fresh air into the box.

The Baranovicht family was sitting in the back of the truck, with the three children sitting between their parents.

"Where are we going?" Moises whispered to his father.

"I'm not sure, but somewhere close to where we will cross the border."

"I'm hot and thirsty," said Yahel.

Her mother, who was sitting next to her, patted her lightly on her sweat soaked head before answering, "We all are, but it shouldn't be much longer, so try to be brave."

Out of the dark, another voice, that of a stranger, spoke to them in a hushed voice.

"When you were getting in the truck, I noticed that you have two boys and a daughter. I'm sure the boys will be fine, but keep your daughter close to you at all times."

"Why is that?" asked Maritza.

"This is my third time to cross the border," replied the unseen man, "and I have seen bad things done to those who trusted the wrong coyotes. This is especially true when there are young girls."

"Why them?" asked Maritza.

"After the girls are across the border, they are sometimes kidnapped by the coyotes and forced to work as prostitutes in the big cities such as Houston and Dallas."

"It's a good thing I'm not a girl," said Salvador, who was intently listening to the conversation between his parents and the stranger.

"Boys are better off," replied the stranger, "but they are sometimes forced to work for the cartels. If they refuse to cooperate they often disappear."

123

"Thank you for the warning," said Maritza, "I won't forget."

"Your thanks are unnecessary, Senora," said the man in the dark, "just be careful, trust no one, and never let yourself be separated from your children."

During the remainder of the trip, nothing else was spoken between the Baranovichts and the stranger. Hours later, the truck came to a stop next to a lone house which was surrounded by bare and empty lots. Seconds later, the doors to the back of the truck were opened.

"Everybody out and inside the house," they were told by a coyote whose name they had yet to learn.

Shading their eyes from the glare of the sunlight, the riders left the truck and entered the house. The last to enter the house was the Baranovicht family, and what they saw was, as Maritza described it, "Utterly horrible."

The house was small, with two bedrooms which had no doors, a kitchen area with no stove or refrigerator, and a single bathroom with no toilet paper. Trash covered and soiled mattresses hid much of the floor space. Holes in the walls and bars on the windows added to the horror, as did a mixture of dead and live roaches and rodent droppings. Future investigation revealed the only source of water was the bathroom sink and the uncovered toilet tank. There was no electricity, and filthy sheets and blankets the only possible means of privacy.

After the men left, someone tried to open the doors to the outside, but discovered the doors had been locked from the outside. Several hours would pass before the coyotes returned with boxes of food and bottled water. When they were asked how long they would be kept in the house, Hector harshly responded, "Until we decide the time is right."

That time wouldn't arrive until two days later, during which time very little food and water was brought to the house…and the doors stayed locked. To Gerardo, the house was even more wretched than where he had been imprisoned.

It was close to the middle of the night, and a restless Maritza was still awake when she heard the familiar sound of the truck stopping outside the house. Nudging her husband awake, she told him, "I think they're coming for us. Why else would they be here this early in the morning?"

She was proven correct when the door was opened and the nameless man announced, "You have five minutes to pack your   things and get in the truck. Any of you who can't do that will be left behind."

Moises and Salvador, who had rushed to fill their collection of empty water bottles, were the last people to climb in the truck. If their parents hadn't refused to let the doors shut until they were on board, they would have been left behind.

Once again the people in the truck were forced to sit in the darkness with no clue to how long they would be kept there. After about forty minutes of bouncing down a pothole filled road, the truck came to a stop. Seconds later the doors were opened.

"Get out, make a single line, and stay quiet," they were told.

Moments later, led by Hector using a flashlight to see by, the line of people was walking north and in the direction of the Rio Grande. The second coyote, also holding a flashlight, was the last person in the line.

After hours of a long cruel walk over rough terrain with only a few brief stops to rest, they were brought to stop. Ahead of them, somewhere in the dark and beyond the curtain of heavy brush, they could hear moving water.

"Stay here and stay quiet," Hector said before both of the coyotes turned off their flashlights and disappeared.

"Are we there?" asked Yahel after they were gone.

"Hush," admonished her mother, "they'll hear you."

Seconds later, she noticed her two other children had vanished into the darkness.

"Where are Salvador and Moises?" she frantically asked her barely visible husband.

"They're up towards the front of the line, giving out our water to the others," he replied.

"Sometimes," she told him, "I think we merely have good sons, but at times like this, I think they're very special."

"A gift from their mother," he replied.

Crouched in hiding by the river's bank, the coyotes were waiting for another gift. After reaching the bank of the river and exchanging a quick flash of light with their comrades on the other side, the two coyotes waited while a man waded across the river. He was trailing a rope behind, a rope which was attached to a mesquite tree on the far side. When he reached the bank and the rope was securely tied to a second mesquite tree, Hector returned to the people waiting in the dark.

"A rope has been stretched across the river," he told them in a tone of voice that sounded like both a threat and a warning. "When you enter the water, keep both hands on the rope at all times. If you lose your grip on the rope and get carried downstream, there's nothing we do to help you."

Not expecting any questions, and not getting any, he continued his instructions.

"The water is higher and faster than usual. Because there may be things coming at you while you're in the river, face upstream so that you can see them coming. That way you may be able to dodge what's coming at you before it can hit you."

Moments later, at intervals designed to prevent too much strain being placed on the rope, the people began entering the water one at a time. Only Yahel and her father were allowed to enter the water together. Salvador deliberately entered the water in front of his mother. When he was halfway across, and judged that it would be difficult for the coyotes on either bank to see him, he planted his feet against the current and stood in place until she caught up to him.

"Thank you," she whispered to him as he took the heavy back pack from her, "I'm not sure I could have held onto the rope much longer."

After the last person had climbed onto dry land, they were immediately formed into to a line and headed inland. The Baranovichts were placed at the back of the line. Within an hour the rising sun and the arid air had dried out their wet clothes. During the following hour, that water was replaced by sweat mixed with dust kicked up by the people walking in front of them.

It was an excruciating walk on thin rough trails covered in loose rocks with thorn covered bushes hanging over the trail and cactus plants reaching out for their legs. The morning temperature had hovered around 90 degrees, with humidity reaching nearly the same figure. By noon, the temperature was over 100 degrees and rising. To the people in the line, the simple act of walking was turning into a challenge just to put one foot in front of the other.

Never letting them stop to rest, and forcing them to drink water while they walked, the coyotes seemed unconcerned for the welfare of anyone. No bathroom breaks were even mentioned or needed. Everyone in the line had sweated out any excess water, and half of them were now feeling the effects of dehydration. Even the two coyotes, who had been at their trade for years and were more accustomed to such harsh conditions, were beginning to show signs of becoming dehydrated.

The Baranovichts, fearing some sort of reprisal, had remained silent during the long trek from the river. It was someone else, possibly the mysterious man who had spoken to them in the darkness of the truck, who dared to challenge the two coyotes.

"We must stop to rest," he told them, "unless you don't care if we live or die."

"Soon," replied Hector in a less than sympathetic voice, "only a little more to go."

He might have said more except for the sound of a low flying plane overhead.

"Hide," Hector shouted at the group of startled people.

Within seconds, everyone had rushed from the trail and sought hiding places under the thick clumps of brush on either side of the path. To their surprise, the Baranovichts found themselves sharing a hiding place with Hector.

"Do you think they saw us?" Maritza asked him.

"There's no way to tell," he answered, "they are smart and they play this game of hide and seek very well. Sometimes, when they spot the illegals, they fly off as if they had seen nothing. They don't want their prey to scatter into the brush before men waiting on the ground are ready to close the trap."

"What do you think we should do if we are found?"

"You have several choices. Either run, stay hidden where you are, or give up."

"I don't think…"

The plane was back and flying low enough that the people on the ground could clearly see the face of a man looking down at them.

When it had passed, Hector rose to his feet and casually shook the sand off his clothes. Seconds later the Baranovichts did the same.

"It's time for you to decide what to do," Hector told them.

"We'll run," Gerardo told him.

"Then run to the south, in the direction we came from," he advised them. "They usually concentrate their search to the north, the direction most people will run. And don't forget your water because you'll probably die without it."

With their mother leading them and the father trailing behind them, the Baranovicht family ran. They ran under a burning sun. They ran until their legs were on the verge of collapsing. When one of them fell down, the others got the fallen one upright. They ran until their lungs were bursting. When they could run no more, they stumbled and crawled off the trail and under some heavy brush, desperate to take advantage of the little shade it provided.

Finally, miles from where the plane's pilot had seen them, they stopped. They had been in a brutal race for their freedom and they had won ...temporarily.

They stayed where they were until late in the afternoon, and until their water, the few bottles remaining that Salvador and Gerardo hadn't given away earlier, had run dry. Not knowing where they were, but certain they needed to go north or northeast, they began walking, keeping the sun on their left to ensure they were northward bound. As they walked, the high brush and mesquite trees were gradually replaced by sparse grasses and undulating country filled with deep dry creek beds which sometimes forced them to climb out of on their hands and knees. Twice they crossed dirt roads, but dared not follow them. Once they heard the drone of a plane and hid in a shallow creek bed hardly suitable to hiding a rabbit. Hungry and thirsty, they spent the night there, with Gerardo and his sons taking turns guarding against rattlesnakes and brown scorpions.

At sunrise they were on their feet and moving once again to the north. After stumbling along blindly for countless hours under a relentless sun and a cloudless sky, they came to an asphalt road. It was there that Maritza and Gerardo decided that they could go no further. Had it been just them, they may have continued the torturous walk, but they had to accept the hard fact that unless they got help, unless they got water, neither they nor their children who had struggled so bravely, were likely to survive.

"Your mother and I think that staying here on the side of the road where we can be found is our only hope," Geraldo told the children, "and that means we will probably get caught and returned to Nicaragua, but that's better than dying."

"We have done what we could," their mother told them, "and you have been brave and strong, but now we must put our destiny in the hands of God."

It might have been luck, or it might have been Divine Providence, but less than twenty minutes later they could hear the sound of an approaching car. Of the five people lying by the side of the road, it was Maritza who found the strength to rise to her knees and turn toward the approaching car. Hours later, Maritza would be told by the driver, "All of you were so caked with dust and dirt that you blended in with the ground, and if you hadn't been upright, I doubt I would have seen you."

When the car came to a stop and the driver emerged, Maritza could see that he was tall, about thirty years old, and wearing a dress shirt and grey pants. He was also unarmed and seemed to have a concerned look on his face. Relieved by his non-threating appearance, but still slightly worried about his reason for stopping, she stood silently until he reached her side.

"Can you help my family?" Maritza begged, "Please, give them water."

Barely able to push air through her parched lips, her words were almost inaudible.

The man paused for a moment while studying her face and trying to understand what she was saying. It was obvious that she was in bad shape, but why, he wondered, is she out here in the middle of nowhere? When he saw her turn her face away from his and point a finger behind her, he could see a man struggling to get to his hands and knees. Three other people, all of them motionless and seemingly near death, were lying feet away from the struggling figure. Seeing them, seeing what had to be a family, brought him to the sudden realization that he was looking at illegal immigrants.

"They must have gone through hell to get from the river to here," he thought with a mixture of both admiration for their bravery and sympathy for their unmistakable suffering.

His job had taken him to this area of south Texas numerous times, and he knew it was one of the more popular areas used by illegal immigrants attempting to get to the United States. He was also aware that some of them could be dangerous if confronted with the prospect of being caught by the either the Border Patrol, local authorities or someone who was a threat to them.

Seeing the near death condition of the woman and the four others erased from his mind any possibility they could be a threat to him or anyone else.

"Yes," he replied, and saying nothing else, moved to the smallest figure.

What he saw when he looked at the face of the fragile young girl was something which would haunt his memory for years afterwards. The girl's face was severely sunburned and her lips were parched and swollen. Her swollen tongue was pushing against her teeth and her breathing came in short wheezes. A quick visual examination of the others showed that they were nearly as bad off.

It took about ten minutes for him to get all of them into his air conditioned Astro van. The youngest, the girl, was placed across the middle seat with her head in her mother's lap. The father took the front seat, while the two boys sat in the rear of the van. A single half empty soft drink was the only form of liquid in the van. When the man handed it to her, Maritza placed the bottle against her daughter's lips and began to drip the precious liquid into her mouth.

"Drink, little Yahel," she implored, "drink."

It could have been that she heard her mother's voice…or maybe it was her instinct to survive, but regardless of the cause, Yahel lifted her head ever so slightly, pressed her lips against the mouth of the bottle, and began to swallow the sweet orange liquid. When the bottle was empty, she opened her eyes and mouthed the word, "Good."

By that time, the driver, ignoring the speed limit, had the van doing eighty-five miles an hour and was within ten miles of a former Holiday Inn which was now a cheap 'mom and pop' motel. The driver knew the motel's restaurant had been shut down for years, but that simple foods and drinks could still be ordered at the bar. It was a place with few patrons, very cold air conditioning, and a loud female bartender with all the charm and grace of a drill sergeant. It was also the only possible "oasis" within ten more miles, and his absolute favorite place to stop in that area of southwest Texas.

Within a minute after arriving at the motel, the driver, carrying the limp girl in his arms, burst through the front door of the motel and into the part of the restaurant which had been converted to a bar.

"I need help," he shouted.

There were three people in the saloon. Denise, the motel's owner and bartender, was the only one he recognized, and the first one to respond to his call for help by rushing from behind the bar.

134

"It's bad," he told her as he felt a slight trembling coming from the little girl in his arms, "and I'm afraid she may be on the verge of having a sun stroke."

Denise placed her hand on the girl's forehead and felt the killing heat through her fingers.

"Come with me," Denise ordered as she headed for the doorway which separated the saloon from her living quarters.

"Give her to me," she said as she stepped into the bathtub and turned on the shower.

Denise held Yahel in her arms under the shower for almost half an hour as her little body slowly recovered from her ordeal.

When she was able to stand on her feet, Denise helped her out of the bathtub, and with Maritza's help, dried her off with a towel.

Denise had lived in that part of Texas for over twenty years, and during that time, she had seen and helped her fair share of people suffering from sunstroke. She also knew at what point they were out of the woods or when they weren't.

"Your little girl is a fighter," she told Maritza, "she's going to be okay, but make sure she drinks plenty of water."

Maritza could only respond with a nod of her head before she reached out and embraced the dripping wet woman standing in front of her.

"You're welcome," said Denise as she returned the embrace.

While Yahel was being tended to, the driver was busy seeing that the other members of her family were given food, water, and ice filled bar towels to wrap around their necks. He was helped by the two men who had been sitting at the bar when he entered the saloon.

When he had first seen the two burly truck drivers, both of whom could have been NFL lineman, he was concerned that given the anti-Mexican sentiments of so many people in southwest Texas, they might be trouble. As it turned out, his concern was laid to rest when they helped the people in the van into the saloon. Later, it was these same men who offered to pay for the food the family ate, and to take the entire family anywhere between there and Amarillo…along with a promise to find them work and a place to stay.

The driver knew those offers, if accepted, carried with them a considerable risk to the truck drivers. If they were unlucky enough to be caught transporting, or even helping 'wet backs,' the law could be hard on them. Hard enough to cost them not just their jobs, but possibly, jail time and a hefty fine.

To the driver, those men, and their offer, symbolized the truest spirit of America.

It was a fast four hours before the Baranovicht family was deemed strong enough to travel. During that time, Maritza was able to explain to her new friends that she and her family were from Nicaragua and not Mexico, and that their only need was to get to relatives living in San Marcos. The driver knew the town, and although it would take him slightly out of his, way, insisted that they stay with him. After a series of hugs all around and some heart felt 'thank you for your kindness' the revitalized Baranovichts were back in the van and on their way to San Marcos.

CHAPTER 16

As much as they had loved their stay on the beach, they knew it had to end. It was the evening before their departure, and all of them were gathered around a burning log, and for the first time, talking with each other about the future.

"What will you do when we get across the border?" Carolina asked.

Her question was directed at Julio.

"I'll work at whatever job I can find, but I want to learn to be a mechanic. After I make enough money, I plan to start dating American girls until I find myself a good wife."

When his teasing comment failed to get the reaction he wanted from Solidad, he asked her what her plans were.

"I'm going to go to college," she answered, "and after that I'm going to be a teacher...but I can't imagine where I could find anyone I would want to marry."

She added a little emphasis to her statement by punching Julio on the arm.

Pepe then announced that he wanted to be policeman or a baseball player. Carolina wasn't sure what she wanted to do, but, following her sister's lead she told them, "Being a teacher would be a good thing."

When they were finished talking, Julio thought it might be the right time to ask a question which had been on his mind from the time he had met them.

"You've told me you were raised by your grandparents, but you've said nothing about your parents."

He was looking into the fire as he spoke, but Solidad knew without a doubt he was talking only to her.

"Years ago, they were in the mountains with the rebels during the war against Somoza," she told him with a slight catch in her voice. "They were killed when some of Somoza's troops, led by a group of Americans, surprised the camp. It was never proven, but the rumor was that the Americans were working for the CIA."

Having heard enough, and not wanting any of them to fully relive such a heart breaking time, Julio sought to change the subject.

"When you get to Texas, where will you go?"

"My mother's brother flew combat missions for the contra-revolutionaries, but months before the war ended, he made his way to San Antonio. After a time, the American embassy gave him political asylum. He's promised to help us become citizens, and I'm sure that if I ask him, he'll also help a certain bad boy from El Salvador."

"He sounds like a good man and a good uncle," said a pleased Julio.

"I think he is," she replied, "and I also think it's a good time for all of us to go to sleep."

Late that night, after Carolina and Pepe were soundly sleeping, Solidad and Julio were sitting next to each other, facing the water and with their backs against a large log. In front of them, a small fire was casting a golden-orange glow. Overhead, in the cloudless sky, a full moon bathed them in light.

"Look," said Solidad as she pointed to where small waves were gently pushing against the shore line, "look at those sparkles."

When Julio looked at the water, he could see that there was something sparkling in the waves when they curled onto the sand.

"That's amazing," he told her, "unbelievable."

"It's beautiful," she replied, "like you."

"My Solidad is like the fire," he whispered as he drew her even closer, "soft and warm."

Moments later, after putting more driftwood on the fire, they fell asleep in each other's arms.

In the morning, Solidad was packing their things when Julio walked over to Chico and tied a piece of rope to the dog's collar. She was puzzled by his action because it was the first time she had seen him put any kind of restraint on the dog.

"Why are you putting a rope on ol' Chico?"

"I have to take him to his new home," replied Julio.

The dejected look on his face told her that, for once, he wasn't teasing her.

"You can't do that to him," she replied as the thought crossed her mind that Julio might be selling him, "we need him to protect us."

"I have to," said Julio without looking at her. "He can't go with us because he won't be allowed on buses or trains, and most people driving cars or trucks won't stop when they see him."

"We can walk," said Solidad,

"It's too far to walk and would take too long," he replied. "We have to leave him here for his own good."

Solidad couldn't deny the truth of his words. She was well aware, that even by using trains or catching rides, they only had enough money between them to barely keep from starving before they reached Texas.

"Are you selling him to someone?" she asked, "because if you are I'll…"

"I would never sell Chico, but I found a family in town who wants him. They're good people with lots of kids for him to take care of."

"Can you do it before Pepe and Carolina wake up?"

"I'll take him now," Julio replied as he finished tying the rope to Chico.

Minutes later they were gone.

Long before they made it through Mexico and to the border city of Reynosa, Solidad had to admit that Julio had been right about leaving Chico behind. There wouldn't have been any way for a dog his size to travel on the top of the train's box cars crowded with hundreds of people. Taking Chico with them would have made the very difficult journey virtually impossible.

From the day they had left home, Solidad, Pepe, and Carolina were prepared for hardships, but what they had to endure as they moved northward would have been impossible for them to have imagined. Only Julio, who had done it before, had known to expect the mind burning sun and the long stretches of time with barely enough food and water. It was his strength that secured them a safer place near the center of the train's shaking box cars. Other people sitting along the sides of the box cars were injured or killed when they were unable to hold on to the few available hand holds.

When the trains stopped, it was Julio who dared to scramble off the train and return with food and water, often only a few strides in front of the gangs of thieves who made the trains' stopping places their private hunting grounds.

Now, only a river separated the four of them from their destination, and a chance at a better life. And as she had many times before, Solidad relied on Julio for a plan which would get them safely across the river.

"Even if we had the money to pay them," Julio told them, I wouldn't want to use the coyotes. They can't be trusted to keep their word. They'll make wonderful promises, take the money, and then do nothing. Another problem is the Federales. The worst of them, the most corrupt and ruthless, work the border towns. They look for people like us, and when they find them, they are worse than the coyotes. They arrest anybody they want to, especially young girls who they use until they're tired of them, and then sell them to whore houses. Because they own the lawyers and judges, they have no fear of the law. They kill, they kidnap, and they torture, with no fear of being prosecuted."

"So what do we do?" asked a suddenly frightened Carolina.

Julio wished he had a good answer to her question, the same question he had been pondering for days. He had been able to think of only one plan, and it was far from perfect. A year earlier, a similar plan had worked for himself and his brother when they crossed the river, but they had been lucky to get as far as they did.

"We let the coyotes lead us to the best place to get across, and then we use it."

"When do we go," asked an excited Pepe.

"We can cross the river in either the daytime or at night. We'd have a better chance of not being caught if we cross the river at night, but once we got on dry land, we'd have nothing to see by accept for moonlight."

"I can see good at night," said Pepe, "I don't need the moon."

"That's great, but the Border Patrol can see better," Julio replied. "They've got these eye glasses they use to see in the dark and other weird stuff that sees heat."

"Are you sure about that," asked a doubtful Solidad, "or are you just trying to scare us?"

"I'm sure that's how my brother and I were caught. After we crossed the river, we thought no one could possible find or catch us, not in country so huge, but they were waiting in the dark for us. While we were in the detention center, we learned that because of their night glasses, they were probably watching us from the time we got in the river. All they had to do was wait for us to come to them."

"So," said Solidad, "what does our great leader think we should do?"

Julio knew she said what she did because she was trying to lighten the mood for the benefit of Caroline and Pepe, so he replied to her playful sarcasm with some of his own.

"An angel like you can spread your wings, fly to San Antonio, and then wait there for us mortals to join you."

Carolina, growing increasingly impatient to hear Julio's real plan, then broke up their light hearted banter.

"Julio," she announced as she crossed her arms in front of her chest and stuck out her jaw, "Pepe and I are waiting."

Her words were enough to silence Solidad and get Julio back on track.

"Later tonight, after I find out where the coyotes are taking people across the river, we'll walk until we get there. My guess is that we'll be going upriver until we're about five miles out of the city. As soon as the sun is high enough in the sky to heat up the ground and make the Border Patrol's night glasses and heat detecting things useless, we'll start across. Other than that, we'll just have to wait and see."

"Before we do that," said Solidad to Julio "there's something else we need to do, and it's very important."

"And that would be…"

"Get something to eat and find a place to sleep," she answered, "or do you want us to starve to death?"

Within an hour they had found a place to sleep. It was in a broken down Greyhound bus sitting in a junk-filled yard adjoining a small cantina. The proprietor of the cantina, and the owner of the bus, was a kindly old man who only charged them ten cents apiece to share the bus with a dozen other people in their same situation. Solidad was happy to pay his wife an additional two dollars for meals of beans, corn bread, chicken tacos, and a cup of Kool-Aid. She knew she could have purchased the food somewhere else for less money, but it wouldn't have included the free use of soap and the water hose connected to the side of the building."

A few hours before sunrise, after filling some discarded plastic bottles with water, and using the road running parallel to the river to guide them, they began walking to the west. None of them became aware, that from the time they left the bus, they were being watched by two of the *kindly* cantina owner's associates. An hour later, Julio led them off the road and in the direction of the river. At first, the arid ground was absent of anything but rocks and sand, with a sprinkling of weeds and cactus. When it changed to head high brush and mesquite trees, Julio brought them to a stop.

"Stay here and stay quiet," he whispered.

"Where are you going" asked Solidad.

"To check out the river," he replied. "I want to see how high the water is and if there's any movement on the other side."

"Try not to get lost," said Solidad.

Ignoring her comment, Julio slung his bedroll over his shoulder and resumed walking toward the river. Within a few steps he vanished into the darkness. Despite moving more than a few yards at a time before stopping to listen for any sign of danger, it took him less than fifteen minutes before he heard the sound made by moving water. He immediately dropped to his stomach and began slowly crawling toward the sound. Unable to see ahead of him, he crawled through cobwebs that clung to his face, and over stinging fire ant beds. Three times he stopped to extract inch long Mesquite thorns from his hands and arms. When he reached the water's edge, he froze momentarily before crawling backward until he was concealed behind a tree. He stayed in that position for over an hour, neither seeing nor hearing anything of concern.

Waiting patiently for something to happen wasn't one of Solidad's better attributes, and by the time dawn was peeking over the eastern sky, her patience had run out. She was about to wake up Caroline and Pepe and go in search of Julio when she heard footsteps.

Thinking it was Julio, she told herself, "It's about time."

But by the time she realized the sound had come from the direction of the road, and not the river, it was too late. She started to stand up, but before she was halfway to her feet, something struck her on the head and she collapsed on the ground. Barely conscious, she could do nothing but watch as one of the men tied her hands behind her back and another man woke up

Caroline and Pepe by kicking them in their legs. Moments later, their hands were also tied behind their backs.

Still dazed from the blow to the head, Solidad watched as the men began rummaging through their belongings. She could see that they were dressed alike. Black colored pants, checkered shirts, cowboy boots, and straw hats. She didn't see any weapons.

When one of them got to her back pack, he missed the few bills she hidden in the pocket of a blouse, but he found the top to her bathing suit.

"Hey, Manual," he said to the other man as he waved the top in the air, "I think maybe you made a mistake when you told me these were young boys we were after."

In response, Manual reached out, grabbed the top, and moved to Solidad's side. Bending down with one knee on the ground, he reached out a hand, grabbed her by the hair, and jerked her to a sitting position.

"I want you to take off your clothes and put this on for me and Chappo," he told her.

Solidad responded by spitting in his face. Manuel responded by driving his fist into her face. The blow opened up an inch long cut above her right eye and sent blood spurting down her face.

"I like a fighter," he told her as he rose to his feet and began unbuckling his pants, "but if you fight me again, my friend Chappo will cut the others."

Hearing his threat, Solidad turned her bloodied face so that she could see the second of their attackers.

Grinning back at her, he removed a pocket knife from his jeans pocket, opened it, and held the tip of the blade against Carolina's cheek.

"I will watch while you have your fun with that one," he told Manual, "and when you are done with her, I will have my fun with the little one."

Bound tightly and injured, a helpless Solidad could do nothing. Feeling certain that what was about to happen to her and Caroline would only be the start of the horrors which would come later, she turned her face away from the man called Chappo and closed her eyes.

"Please God," she silently prayed, "let Julio help us."

"Good girl," she heard the man standing above her say.

His words were followed by the sound of rattling coins as his pants fell on the ground by her feet. His mistake, and the same mistake his partner was making, was that he had failed to account for the fourth person they had been following.

Solidad opened her eyes when she heard the man standing over her suddenly scream out in pain.

The rock fired from Julio's sling shot glanced off the bridge of Manual's nose and buried itself in his left eye. The pain which followed caused him to instinctively cover his face with his hands and stagger a step backwards. When he pulled his hands away, his left hand had a marble sized blood covered rock in it. The scream of pain and fury which followed, was the same one which had made Solidad open her eyes.

Hearing his partner's scream, and then seeing his bleeding face and hands, Chappo spun in a half circle while searching with his eyes for who or what had hurt his partner. The first thing he saw was the girl in front of Manuel bringing a knee up to her chest and then kicking him in the groin. The next thing he saw, out of the corner of his eye, was a man running at him with a piece of pipe in his up-raised hand.

Chappo had lived in a violent world for most of his life. He had seen men fight, and he had seen them die. He had learned from this that survival was often the result of good luck or being smart enough to know when to fight and when not to fight. As a result, he had become a man who wasn't overly brave or overly cowardly, but he was practical. These people, the two girls and the boy, had nothing of value except their bodies, and to him, those weren't worth the risk of being injured or killed.

With his partner writhing on the ground, and seeing nothing to gain by fighting someone brandishing a weapon, he held the hand holding the knife over his head and extended the other hand out in front of him.

"No, no, no," he shouted at the man, "we will leave."

"Then do it," Julio replied as he held the piece of pipe in front of the man's face, "but leave the knife behind."

Without another word being spoken between them, Julio watched carefully as the man dropped the knife to the ground before helping the other man to his feet. With the injured man holding up his pants up with one hand, and his other hand holding on to his partner's shoulder for support, both men started moving in the direction of the road. A moment before they were out of sight, they turned their heads in Julio's direction and looked into his eyes. The cold menacing look on their faces made it clear to Julio that if given enough time, a second encounter with them would have an entirely different ending.

After they were out of sight, Julio used the discarded knife to cut the ropes binding Pepe and Carolina before rushing to Solidad's side. With blood dripping from the cut above her eye, and a bluish knot on her forehead, the sight which greeted him was not a pretty one. Only the small smile on her face helped to assure him that she wasn't seriously hurt.

"I shouldn't have left you," he told her.

"I'll forgive you," she replied, "but not until after you cut me lose."

As soon as Julio cut away the rope from her wrists, Solidad stood up and faced him.

"Thank you for saving us," she told him as she put her arms around his neck and hugged him with a strength he hadn't known she possessed. To Julio, despite her wounds and the blood on her face, she was still the most utterly beautiful girl in the world. They were still locked in an embrace when they were joined by Carolina and Pepe.

"I was so afraid they would kill us," said Carolina who was unable to control a slight shaking.

"Not me," said Pepe, "I wasn't afraid because I knew Julio would save us."

"I knew it too," replied Carolina who wasn't about to let her brother think he was braver than she was, "that's why I was only a little afraid."

"I just know that both of you are very brave," said Solidad, "and so is Julio."

"What I know," said Julio as he thought about the menacing look on the faces of the two men, "is that we need to get out of here before those men you two aren't afraid of come back with some of their friends."

He got no argument from the others, and after treating Solidad's cut by pressing a cloth against it until the bleeding stopped, they set out for the river. When they were near enough to hear it, they did what Julio had previously done. They crawled on their hands until they could see across the river through the brush, but were still far back enough from the water line that they were concealed from sight by anyone on the other side.

"Now what do we do?" asked Solidad.

"I'd like to wait here long enough to make sure there's no one on the other side, "but we don't have time to do that," Julio replied, "we have to go across now, before those men come back looking to get even."

"How deep is the water?" asked Pepe.

"I'll let you know after I get to the other side."

He was rewarded for his answer by getting a hard stare from Pepe's older sister.

"It shouldn't take me more than a few minutes to get across," he told her, "if there are men waiting on the other side, at least I'll be the only one they catch."

His explanation of why he should go alone was so persuasive, that seconds later, four brave young people with little to lose and so much to gain, were less than a foot apart when they stepped in the river.

CHAPTER 17

The crossing went smoothly, with none of them falling into the water which never rose above their waist. After reaching the far side, Julio scouted out the area and then waved to the others to leave the river. About a hundred yards inland, Julio had them stop to rest and to 'look and listen.'

While they were resting, Julio said, "From now on, we stay off of the trails as much as possible, but we'll use them when the land is so rough that there's no other choice."

As it turned out, when they tried to travel off trail, the rocky terrain tore up their feet, cactus plants ripped at their clothes and legs, and thorns from mesquite trees slowed their progress to a crawl. Despite the increased possibility of being discovered by the Border Patrol, they were forced to use the well-worn trails.

They walked for several hours, only stopping for a few brief moments to get their bearing and to take sips of their dwindling water supply. The only frightening moment occurred when they thought the sound made by a herd of javalinas might have been made by the Border Patrol. That sound sent them scrambling off the trail in search of a place to hide.

When they glimpsed the javalinas running through the brush and realized their mistake, they shared a short laugh before they resumed walking. They had no way of knowing the javalinas, that could have been as dangerous to them as people might be, were fleeing from the presence of two humans.

Minutes later, they were caught totally off guard when a man and a woman, both in uniform and armed, stepped out in front of them.

"Stop where you are," the man told them in Spanish.

Then, pointing the shot gun he was holding at the ground, the man indicated he wanted them to sit down. After hesitating for a moment, and realizing that both avenues of escape were cut off, Julio nodded at Solidad, silently telling her that there was nothing they could do but comply.

Prior to joining the county sheriff's department, Jesse Molina, had spent two years on a baseball scholarship at Brooks County Junior College. When injuries to his throwing arm and knee ended any chance of a future in baseball, he attempted to join the army, but flunked the army's physical because of the same bad knee. Months later, after a night spent in the county jail for being drunk and disorderly, he did something highly unusual. He applied for a deputy's job with the same Brooks County Sheriff's Department.

After two years on the job, he was teamed up with Meagan Hergert, his current partner.

After graduating from high school in Nederland, Texas, Meagan Hergert had tried the college life, but dropped out as a result of sheer boredom, poor grades, and a few too many wild parties. Because of a failed romance which left her broke, carless, and stranded in McAllen, she took a low paying part time job at a day care for kids. After a chance conversation with one of the kid's mother who worked as a dispatcher at the county jail, she went to work there as a jailer. When the county needed more people in the field to combat the rise of illegal immigrants streaming across the border, she applied for one of the positions, but was turned down because she lacked the one essential quality necessary to the job. She wasn't bi-lingual. Smart, and with a talent for languages, she enrolled in night school. Six months after enrolling, and now able to speak Spanish to a reasonable degree, she was hired as a deputy sheriff.

While Jesse kept his eye on the four illegals, Meagan began searching through their meager belongings. She was looking for drugs, weapons, or any other signs of criminal activity. Finding nothing of interest in the first three bundles except for the swim suits, she moved to Julio's bedroll, opened it up and dumped the contents at her feet. The first thing that caught her eye was a piece of pipe that could have no other purpose other than to be used as a weapon. There was also a sling shot. Catching illegals with weapons for protection was not an unusual thing, but the weapons usually consisted of knives, hand guns, or brass knuckles. The sling shot and the piece of pipe were a first.

She looked at Julio and her immediate impression was, "There's no way in hell he's a coyote, and if he's a criminal, he's certainly an unusual one."

"Why are you carrying a pipe and a sling shot?" she asked Julio, "you planning to do some hunting or plumbing?"

Before he could reply, Pepe blurted out, "Julio saved us from the men who hurt my sister."

Meagan had asked the question in Spanish, and was surprised to hear a reply in English. A lot of the older illegals, usually the ones who had been here before, spoke some English, but it was unusual for the younger illegals to speak even the broken English the boy had used.

Because of having followed procedure when first dealing with illegals by searching them for weapons, she hadn't taken a close look at any of them. Now she did.

She saw that the two boys and the younger girl had small amounts of blood on their clothes, but no signs or indications of a wound. The same was not true of the older girl. She had dried blood on her clothes, in her hair, and a cut above an eyebrow. She also had a swollen eye from what had to have been caused by a recent blow to her face.

"Do you need a doctor?" Meagan asked in Spanish, and as it had been with the younger boy, she was answered in English.

"No," Solidad answered, "but thank you for asking."

"You and your brother speak English well," said Meagan. "How did you learn the language?"

"So does my sister," replied Solidad. "Years ago, my grandparents knew they wanted us to come to the United States, and that it would be easier for us if we learned your language before we got here. They persuaded our parish priest, who was educated in the U.S., to teach us the language of the north."

Jesse had stayed back, watching the four illegals for a sign that they would be trouble. At first glance, they looked harmless, but he knew that was an assumption that had got other deputies hurt. Now, certain after the search of their belonging that they didn't pose a threat, he took over the questioning.

"Where are you from?" he asked Julio.

Solidad, knowing Julio understood very little English, answered for him.

"Julio's from El Salvador. My brother, sister and I are from Nicaragua."

"What did you expect to do after you got here?

"Julio wants to be a mechanic, and my brother wants to be a baseball player," she replied, "my sister and I will go to college to be teachers."

Jesse was not only impressed by her answer and the conviction in her voice, he also believed that given the opportunity, she would do exactly what she said she would.

"If you have any chance of staying in this country, you have to have a sponsor," he told her, "someone who is legally in this country, someone who can help you."

"I know about the sponsors," said Solidad. "We have an uncle in San Antonio who will sponsor us."

Meagan had been listening and suspected where her partner was going with this line of questioning. When he asked the girl, "Can you prove it?" she

KNEW he was thinking of doing something which could seriously backfire on both of them…if they got caught.

Solidad, not positive her uncle was a legal immigrant despite what he had written in his letters, hesitated before answering the question. She didn't want to cause her uncle trouble, but if she didn't answer his question, she was positive she would be throwing away the possibility of any of them staying in the United States.

"I have memorized his address and phone number," she reluctantly answered, "he was a fighter pilot in the contra air force and has political asylum."

"I need that information," Jesse told her as he removed a pad and pencil from his shirt pocket.

As she was giving him the information, Solidad said a silent prayer that she had done the right thing.

Jesse had always been emotionally conflicted when he caught the illegals and had to turn them over to the Border Patrol for deportation. He had sworn an oath to faithfully serve and protect, and he took that oath seriously. But his mother was Hispanic, and he remembered how his grandparents, who were illegals before becoming citizens, had for years lived in fear they would be discovered and deported. He was now caught on the proverbial fence separating his conscience and his sworn duty. He had to make a decision whether to ignore that oath, or end the dream of the four people sitting before him. He chose to keep their dream alive.

"Wait here with them while I go to the car," he told Meagan as he turned to walk away, "I should be back in an hour, tops."

"You're crazy," she shouted after him, "but it's a good crazy."

After he was gone, Meagan could see that the group of people she was guarding was growing more nervous with each passing moment.

"I would be too," she thought, "and scared out of my ever lovin' wits."

Noticing that the two youngest in the group seemed the most apprehensive, she moved over next to them, and sat down with her arm around Carolina's shoulder.

"Don't be afraid." she said loudly enough that the others could hear her, "my partner and I are going to do everything we can to help you."

Her words had the calming effect she hoped for.

"Are you Mexican?" Carolina asked her.

Meagan had to laugh at the question, but she understood it. With her deep brown hair and brown eyes, combined with her year round tan from working hundreds of hours under the southwest Texas sun, it wasn't the first time she had been asked that question.

"No, Sweetheart," she replied, "I'm sort of a mix of Irish, Polish, and who knows what else, but I was born in New Jersey, so I think of myself as just an American."

"I want to be an American like Mickey Mantle," said Pepe, "and play for the Yankees."

"And I hope you do," Meagan replied, "because they're my favorite team."

For the next half hour all of them engaged in a light conversation which ended when Jesse returned. He was carrying with him an Igloo cooler and a First Aid kit. The cooler contained bottles of water and oranges covered in ice. Ten minutes later, half the water and oranges were gone, and the ice was going fast. Now it was time for him to explain what he had planned for them.

"After we leave, I want you to stay hidden, but close by here. Get some rest, but don't go out of the sound of my voice. There should be enough water to last you until later tonight when I will come back to get you. Understand?"

"We understand," said Solidad, "but why are you doing this? I have always heard the Border Patrol people are mean."

"Meagan and I aren't Border Patrol," he replied, "and we are doing this because…well, because…"

Meagan could tell that Jesse was struggling to find an answer to the girl's question, so she answered for him.

"He's doing it because he's a good man with a big heart," she added as she looked at him, "and I guess he's not the only one with a heart problem."

It was the last thing she said until they got back to the car.

"So, Mister Save the World," she asked playfully, "may I ask what kind of trouble you're getting us into?"

"I checked on the name and address of the uncle, and he's for real. He's been working for seven years as an airline mechanic."

"Great," Meagan replied, "but how to you plan to get them together with this uncle? And what do we do if they get caught before we do that?"

"If they stay where they are, they won't get caught. I let the Border Patrol know things are quiet in this sector, and that we'd stay around until after dark."

"Very clever," said Meagan, "but what do we do after we go back to get them?"

"Load 'em up in the back seat and take them to your place."

"My place," replied the truly surprised Meagan. "You want to take them to my place?"

"They'll love it there."

What's wrong with taking them to your apartment?"

"Too many nosey neighbors."

"I see," she replied, "and we wouldn't want our guests to interfere with your poker game."

"That too," admitted a smiling Jesse, "I'd hate to disappoint the guys."

"And what do we do with them when tomorrow rolls around?"

"Not we, me. First thing in the morning I take them to their uncle."

"You don't have a car." said Meagan.

"Sure I do," Jesse said, "we're sitting in it."

"You're going to drive four illegals out of the county, in a county car, and past a dozen patrol cars?"

"Don't you just love a brilliant plan?"

"I'll try to bring something for you to eat when I visit you in the Bexar County lock up."

161

"Make it a DQ hamburger, no onions, and a small file."

"Have you thought about taking them to that safe house in Harlingen?" Meagan asked.

"Surely," said Jess, "You're referring to the same safe house the Feds have under observation twenty-four seven. They'd love to see two county deputies pulling up to the church and dropping off four illegals. We'd be lucky if our next job involved hanging off the back of a garbage truck.

"I need a beer," said Meagan.

"A gentleman never lets a lady drink alone," Jesse replied as he reached into the back seat for their 'reserve' Igloo cooler labeled "For Official Use Only."

CHAPTER 18

Maritza's sister didn't exactly live in San Marcos, but it was close. Following the instructions her sister had given him on the phone, the driver stayed on Interstate 35 until he reached the exit for highway 80. He drove east on 80 for about five miles until he reached FM 1979 on the east side of Martindale. Seconds later, after turning to the right, he was driving between rows of small houses. A crowd of people gathered in front of one of the houses and waving at the van told him he had reached his destination.

"It looks like someone is happy to see you," said the driver as he pulled into the driveway.

"Not as happy as we are to see them," replied Maritza.

It was a sentiment echoed by her entire family.

Even before the driver brought the van to a stop and turned off the motor, the van was being swarmed on all sides. Minutes after the Baranovicht family exited the van, the driver was back on the road. Nearly a half hour went by before his absence was noticed.

Three weeks later, a similar but smaller reunion, was about to take place.

Shortly before 10:00 am, Jesse pulled up to the front of Meagan's house and honked the car horn. Inside the house, Meagan was in the middle of serving a second round of breakfast to her quests.

"Now he's early," she muttered to herself. They had agreed that he would be back at 10:00 am, but with his history of being late to everything, she hadn't expected to see him until 10:30 at the least.

"Time to go," she hollered out to the four people sitting at the kitchen table, "your chariot has arrived."

As one, the four people rose to their feet, and picked up their back packs which had been left by the front door. As they did, Meagan marveled at the transformation they had undergone since the day before.

"Hot showers, good food, clean clothes, and a full night's sleep certainly make a hell of a difference," she told herself.

It was the same conclusion Jesse came to when he saw them walking to the car. To him, Carolina and Pepe, all cleaned up with their hair combed and shiny, looked like typical middle school kids. Solidad had her hair tied back in a ponytail, and was wearing black jeans with a silver studded belt, white tennis shoes, and a pink t-shirt. With the addition of the make-up Meagan had insisted she needed, she could have stepped right into a high school production of *Grease*.

Julio completed the group transformation by wearing a Dallas Cowboy jersey over a pair of faded jeans. Having shaved the light mustache and chin whiskers added significantly to his new 'American' image.

"Well, Mama Meagan, I'd say somebody did a decent job of getting the kids ready."

"You just make sure *you* take good care of them," replied Meagan, "cause if you don't, you'll have to deal with me."

"See you later," replied Jesse as he noticed her eyes beginning to water up.

For the next two hours as Jesse drove north, very little was spoken by anyone in the car. That changed when they reached the outskirts of San Antonio and the car's amazed passengers got their first look at multi-storied skyscrapers jutting into the sky. Within moments, all four of Jesse's passengers started up a constant conversation about what they were seeing. The conversation persisted until the car stopped in front of a brick house several blocks off of State Highway 1604.

Inside the house, Francisco was in a quandary. The man he talked to the previous evening had given him the name Jesse, but he hadn't said anything about what he would be driving. Logically, he had expected to see either a car or a truck, but when the police car stopped in front of the house, his only thought was that something had gone terribly wrong. His apprehension grew even larger when a Sheriff's officer stepped out of the car and began approaching the house. After hearing a knock at the door, Francisco, with his pulse racing, opened front door and stepped out on the porch.

Neither man had a description of the other, but both of them had a reason for treading lightly until they knew for certain who the other man was.

"Can I help you?" Francisco asked rather stiffly.

"You can if you're Uncle Francisco," replied Jesse, "and if you are I've got some people who have come a long way to meet you,"

The smile that appeared on Francisco's face and his suddenly relaxed posture told Jesse he had come to the right house.

Solidad had exchanged several letters with her uncle, but she hadn't seen him or talked to him since she was a small child. She had seen his pictures in her grandparent's house, but those pictures were ten or more years old.

"And people can change in that time," she told herself.

Her worries came to an end when Jesse and the man on the porch began vigorously shaking hands.

"We're home." she said to her brother and sister, "we're finally home."

Summer 1989

It was shortly before noon and hundreds of people lined the main street of the town, all of them eager for the beginning of Martindale's annual Fourth of July parade. Among the crowd were the local Anglo families sitting or standing with families from Mexico and the Central Americas. Many of the children were happily waving small American flags while they waited for the parade to start. Larger flags adorned most of the town's stores and buildings, and a banner declaring Martindale's patriotic spirit was stretched high over the street.

For the Baranovicht family, after living in the United States for a year, the celebration provided them with dual opportunities. First, to celebrate their

166

adopted country's birthday, and secondly, to meet other families and people from Central American countries, and in particular those from Nicaragua.

"How did you meet this new friend of yours?" Maritza asked her husband.

"It just so happens that Francisco and myself share a similar interest in a sporting event," Gerardo replied, "and after I learned he was from Nicaragua, I naturally invited him and his family to join us."

"So, does this sporting event have anything to do with poultry?" questioned Maritza.

She was well aware of her husband's infatuation with cock fighting, and also aware of the small amounts of money tied to betting on favorite birds.

"That could be so," said Gerardo.

"Birds of a feather," replied Maritza, "or should I say 'scoundrels and gamblers of a feather'?"

Gerardo was prevented from laughing at his wife's loving criticism by a voice from behind them.

"He is a scoundrel of the worst kind, Senora, but I, on the other hand, am a man of irrefutable honesty."

Gerardo turned to see a slender man standing behind them.

"Francisco, my friend, said Gerardo, "it is so good to see you."

Maritza's reaction was to turn in her chair and see an adult and four younger people standing behind her.

"You must be Francisco," Maritza said as both she and Gerardo stood up and faced them.

"I am, and these are my nieces Solidad and Carolina, my nephew Pepe, and Solidad's fiancé Julio."

"This is my wife, Maritza," Gerardo told them. "I would introduce you to the rest of my family but they stopped at River Park to look at the river and set up the tables for the picnic we will have after the parade."

"My husband has told me about all of you," said Maritza as she looked at the four young people. "What you did to get to Texas was very brave."

"No more so than what we've heard about you," replied Solidad.

As the parade was about to begin, Salvador, Moises and Yahel walked up to their parents.

"Ah," said Gerardo to Francisco, "here is the rest of my family."

Introductions were quickly made as the parade began to pass in front of them. Candy was thrown from the floats and all of the children, even the teenagers, darted out into the street to get their share of the treats.

During this time, the children from both families cast furtive glances at one another trying to size up each other. Moises' looks tended to centered on Carolina who he thought was especially pretty. He decided he would try to get to know her better as the day went on.

After the parade, while Maritza and Gerardo returned home to get the already prepared food for the picnic, the children along with Francisco walked to River Park. The children were excitedly talking about swimming in the San Marcos River and maybe even trying to float over the dam.

Hours later, tired from swimming and sated with the second round of food provided by the Baranovicht's the group returned to the house to rest and recover from the day's activities and the heat of the sun.

At dusk, the families returned to River Park to watch the fireworks display. The park was crowded with other families there for the same reason. Because of this, none of the adults noticed when Moises and Carolina slipped away from the group and went down to the river's edge.

"Do you ever miss Nicaragua?" Moises asked.

"Sometimes, I do, I certainly miss my grandparents, but here I have been able to get a good education. I love my high school, and after I graduate, I plan to attend Southwest Texas State and get a degree in education."

She then asked the same question of Moises. His reply was that he also, at times, missed Nicaragua and he planned to go back some day to live there.

"That sounds wonderful," said Carolina. "And, who knows, maybe I will go back with you."

Years later, after they were married, they returned several times to Nicaragua. It was during these trips they decided that when the last of their children had finished college they would return to Nicaragua permanently.

Epilogue

Twenty minutes after leaving home I parked my pick-up in front of Jason's Deli and made my way inside. After catching the eye of the manager I was there to meet, I took a seat at an empty table. Several minutes passed before the man was able to join me.

Our meeting had come about after a conversation with my son, Michael, during which he mentioned that his manager where he worked had come to Texas from Nicaragua when he was fourteen. Being the uncontrollable story teller I am, I then told Michael about some of the experiences I had in Nicaragua back in the mid-seventies. Subsequently, Michael relayed my story to Gerardo who then asked if I could write down some of the story to show his family and friends. I did that, and in the process began to formulate in my mind what could be the meat of a sixth book.

We talked for about two hours and what he told me about his early family history, and what they endured before coming to this country, convinced me that there was a story there. For over a year I had hoped to write a book that had some social significance, and not just another bit of light reading, and now I had the source of the material I needed sitting across the table from me.

At the time, the plight and the problems of illegal immigrants was a big part of the local and national news. I was, and have always been, on the side of those people who risked so much to get here. I grew up in a neighborhood with a good number of Mexican families. The Mexican kids were my friends and my playmates, and in my naive mind, the only thing which differentiated them from "us" was the prejudice I occasionally saw. It didn't come so much from the kids in the neighborhood or my classmates, but from the adults and the parents. What I didn't see, and have yet to fully understand, was how deep that prejudice was, or how it slammed shut the doors to the opportunities which were open to 'us.'

Leaving the deli with Gerardo's agreement to be a co-author, all that was left was for me to write the story, and that meant coming up with a beginning. Before I reached home, I had decided on "My name is Gerardo Moises Baranovicht, and this is my story."

Afterward

Immigrants came to this land, first by the hundreds, then by the thousands, and then by the millions. They came by boat, by air, on slave ships, and by walking to the north. They were from Europe, from Asia, from South America, from Africa, from Mexico and Central America. They came from all points of the compass, and for as many reasons. They built our cities, tamed the West, laid the tracks, dug the coal from the mines, and worked the fields which grew the food that came to our tables. They fought our wars, enhanced our culture and language, and enriched the lives of each succeeding generation.

They are our doctors, our ranchers, our teachers, our builders, our poets, our politicians, and our laborers. They are US, and they contributed to making our country the strongest and best country in the world.

Now, there are people who cry out, "Close the border to the people from the south." "Protect our jobs," they say. "Don't come here if you can't speak "our" language." These people, the proud but ignorant people who will not, or cannot embrace our history are, in the opinion of this author, WRONG…and they are not the voice of this nation.

People, Places, Things from the Novel in the order they appear.

People – nonfiction characters from the novel

<u>Gerardo Moises Baranovicht</u> - He collaborated extensively with the author of this book. After coming illegally to this country, he was given political asylum. He is now a manager of a Jason's Deli in San Marcos, TX. He is justifiable proud of his heritage, of his family, and proud to be both an American and a Nicaraguan. After retirement he plans to return to Chinandega. Extraordinary events sometimes produce extraordinary people. He is one of them.

<u>Jose Esteban Lau/Chi Chu Lau</u> - He was much as depicted in this book. He was flamboyant, independent, successful, loyal in his own way, and a confirmed romantic. The mystery surrounding his disappearance, and that of his children, has never been solved.

<u>Emigdio Enrique Baranovicht</u> - father of Enrique Baranovicht. He immigrated to Nicaragua from Belarus.

<u>Mongol invaders</u> – were followers of Genghis Khan who helped establish the Mongol Empire in the 13th century. The empire covered much of Asia and Eastern Europe.

<u>Khans</u> – were the sovereign military rulers of the Mongol Empire.

British – are citizens of Great Britain.

<u>National Revolutionary Army (NRA)</u> – was the military arm of the Kuomintang (the Chinese Nationalist Party) from 1925 until 1947 in the Republic of China.

<u>Chang Kai-Shek</u> – was head of state of the Chinese Nationalist government between 1928 and 1949. He was a Chinese military and political leader who led the National Revolutionary Army for five decades.

<u>General Bai Chongxi</u> – was a Chinese general in the National Revolutionary Army of the Republic of China.

<u>President Hoover</u> – was the 31st president of the United States. He served in that capacity from 1929 – 1933.

<u>Babe Ruth</u> – was a professional baseball player who was well-known for his powerful hitting prowess.

<u>Yankees</u> – are the American League baseball team from New York City.

<u>Christians</u> – are followers of Jesus Christ.

<u>Darwinians</u> – are believers in the theory of evolution.

<u>Petrona Maria Ramos Lau</u> – the wife of Jose Esteban Lau and grandmother of Moises Baranovicht.

<u>Maritza Lau</u> – wife of Enrique Baranovicht. She now lives comfortably in Texas, in her own home near Moises and his family.

<u>Anastasio Somoza DeBayle</u> – a Nicaraguan dictator who was overthrown by the FSLN in 1979, ending the Somoza dynasty,

<u>Anastasio Somoza Garcia</u> – After being elected by an overwhelming vote as president in 1936, Somoza Garcia resumed control of the National Guard and established a dictatorship and family dynasty that would rule Nicaragua for more than 40 years.

<u>Nicaraguan National Guard</u> – troops loyal to Anastasio Somoza and his regime.

<u>Augusto Caesar Sandino</u> - led the Nicaraguan resistance against the United States occupation of Nicaragua in the

1930s. He was a Nicaraguan revolutionary and leader of a rebellion between 1927 and 1933 against the U.S. military occupation of Nicaragua. He was referred to as a "bandit" by the United States government; his exploits made him a hero throughout much of Latin America, where he became a symbol of resistance to United States' domination. He drew units of the United States Marine Corps into an undeclared guerrilla war. Sandino was assassinated in 1934 by National Guard forces of Gen. Anastasio Somoza García, who went on to seize power in a coup d'état two years later.

<u>Karl Marx</u> – a German economist and philosopher. He wrote Das Kapital and The Communist Manifesto. His theories were adopted by different countries, most notably Russia and China.

Socialist Party – a political party that follows the tenets of socialism which supports the idea that businesses should be controlled by the government rather than by individuals or companies.

Nazis – the National Socialist German Workers' Party led by Adolf Hitler that ruled Germany from 1933 – 1945.

<u>Belarusians</u> – citizens of Belarus.

<u>Enrique Baranovicht</u> – The husband of Maritza and father of Salvador, Moises and Yahel. After coming to the United States, he worked at menial jobs. Janitor, garbage man, any work he could find to support his family. He returned to Nicaragua in 1991, and raised fighting rooster. He died at the age of 60.

<u>Catilena Baranovicht</u> - Emidgio's Russian born wife and mother to Enrique.

Salvador Baranovicht – is the first born of Enrique and Maritza Baranovicht and the older brother of Geraldo Moises.

Yahel Baranovicht – is the sister of Salvador and Geraldo Moises.

Sandinistas (FSLN) – is a Nicaraguan democratic socialist political party. The FSLN overthrew Anastasio Somoza Debayle in 1979, ending the Somoza dynasty, and established a revolutionary government in its place. Following their seizure of power, the Sandinistas ruled Nicaragua from 1979 to 1990, first as part of a Junta of National Reconstruction. Following the resignation of centrist members from this Junta, the FSLN took exclusive power in March 1981. They instituted a policy of mass literacy, devoted significant resources to health care, and promoted gender equality.

Contras - A militia, known as the Contras was formed in 1981 to overthrow the Sandinista government and was funded and trained by the US Central Intelligence Agency.

Soviets – was the name given to the political, military, and the people of the former United Soviet Socialist Republic.

David – is a Biblical figure who slew the giant Goliath and later became king of the Israelites.

Goliath – a member of the Philistine army gathered to fight King Saul and the Israelites.

Jerry Waller/Abner/Sarge - A highly decorated Viet Nam veteran, he fought in several of the most intensive battles of the war. After being discharged from the army he returned to Lively Grove, IL, and settled into the life of a farmer and a father of three girls. One of them, Marcie Coryell, is married to my son and the mother of two, five year old Dylan and two year old Myra. Their grandfather "Abner" had no connection to the CIA.

<u>Leonard Parker/Poochie</u> - He served with the author in the Air Force in the 60's. Truly fast and a gifted all-round athletic, his hand-eye coordination and his sense of humor were second to none.

<u>Steven Smith/Slim</u> – the Smiths, Pat and Dick, have been friends to the Coryell family from the time our kids played soccer and baseball together. A graduate of Texas A&M, Steven is a Lt. Commander in the Navy, and pilots H-60 helicopters off the decks of aircraft carriers. He lives in Jacksonville, FL with his wife Alyssa and their three children. Stay dry Steven.

<u>Willie Lessert</u> - A Sioux Indian and an Air Force medic, Bill served with the author in Alaska. He was unusually quiet, witty, and stoic, but always listened to when he spoke. He was an excellent self-taught guitar player who spent hours entertaining his buddies.

<u>Ron Hall</u> - A "Manchu" who served with Jerry from the time they met in boot camp. He passed away at his home in Ohio.

<u>The Three Stooges</u> – were an U.S. comedy trio of the mid-20s known for their physical farce and slapstick.

<u>John Wayne</u> – an American actor who graced the big screen from 1930 to 1979. He is the author's favorite actor, of whom he often does impressions.

<u>Mayans</u> – were members an ancient civilization that was centered in Guatemala and reaching its peak in power and influence around the 6th century A.D.

Bravo Company, 9th Infantry Regiment, 25th Infantry Division – was trained intensively in jungle warfare and Asian languages in preparation for involvement in the Viet Nam conflict.

<u>Manchus</u> – were people who conquered China in the 1600s and ruled for over 250 years. They were worthy adversaries and much feared in battle.

<u>Custer</u> – was an American general in the 1800s who fought in the Civil War and was later assigned to the western territories. In 1876 he led his 210 men at the Battle of Little Big Horn where the entire regiment was decimated.

<u>VC</u> – an acronym for the Viet Cong, the army in Viet Nam and Cambodia that fought the United States and South Vietnam from 1959 through 1975.

<u>Father Rosales</u> – his name was borrowed from Reuban Gonzales. He lives in Beaumont, TX, works as a bartender in a upscale restaurant, goes to college, and is a friend of our daughter Christi. His parents were from El Salvador, but he was born and raised in Maryland.

<u>Castro</u> – was the leader of the revolution against Baptista in Cuba in 1959. He became the president/dictator of the island nation in 1976 and served in that capacity until 2008

<u>Baptista</u> – was a political leader of Cuba who ruled the country twice. He ruled from 1933 – 1944 and from 1952 – 1959. His last regime was a dictatorial one and

rife with persecution and terror. He was ousted from power in 1959.

<u>Communists</u> – people who adhere to the ideology of Communism that espouses public ownership and community control of property and the economy.

<u>Carolina</u> - Nicaraguan born, she, like her husband Moises, came to this country as an illegal. The mother of Iesha, Alyssa, and Ezekiel, she might be described as a "soccer mom." She's much as depicted in the book, but more.

<u>Coyotes</u> – are human traffickers who smuggle illegal aliens into the United States.

<u>Wet backs</u> – is a derogatory term denoting any illegal alien from Mexico who arrived in the United States by swimming or wading across the Rio Grande.

<u>Federales</u> – is a term designating the Mexican federal police.

<u>Border Patrol</u> – are people belonging to the law enforcement arm of the United States charged with preventing illegal immigrants from entering the country.

<u>Meagan Hergert</u> - Meagan is the older daughter of Florrie O'Keefe, my wife's sister. Before becoming an elementary school teacher in Beaumont, TX she worked in a day care center. She loves to laugh, has a compassion for all things great and small, and appreciates a 'cold one.'

<u>Mickey Mantle</u> – was a baseball Hall of Famer who is considered to be the greatest switch hitter ever. His entire career was played for the New York Yankees.

Francisco Ramos - A pilot in the contra air force during the war between the contras and the Sandinistas, he immigrated (political asylum) to the United States in 1982. He introduced Carolina to Gerardo.

Places

Hong Cong - is a city on the southern coast of China at the Pearl River Estuary and the South China Sea.

South China Sea – is part of the Pacific Ocean, encompassing an area from the Singapore and Malacca Straits to the Strait of Taiwan.

Pacific Ocean – is the largest ocean on earth located between Asia and the Americas.

Hawaii – is the fiftieth state of the United States. It is a series of islands located in the Pacific Ocean.

San Francisco – was founded in 1776. It is considered the cultural, financial and commercial center of northern California.

Mexico – is the southernmost country in North America.

Nicaragua – is the largest country in Central American located between Honduras and Costa Rica.

United States – is a country in North America with Canada as its northern border and Mexico as its southern border.

London – is the capital city of England.

Canton – is the capital city of Guangdong province in South China.

Longquan – is a city in the southwest of Zhejiang Province, China.

<u>China</u> – is the world's most populous country and is located in East Asia.

<u>Beijing</u> – is the capital city of China.

<u>Pearl Harbor</u> – is located on the island of Oahu, Hawaii. It has a natural harbor lagoon making a perfect port location.

<u>City by the Bay</u> – is the nickname of San Francisco, California.

<u>Chinandega</u> – is a city in northwestern Nicaragua and the home of the Lau and Baranovicht families.

<u>Our Lady Santa Ana Colonial Church</u> – is located in Chinandega and was established in 1751. It's original building was severely damaged by an earthquake in 1885 and was rebuilt at its current location on the city square.

<u>Belarus</u> – is a country in central Europe that shares borders with Russia, Ukraine, Poland, Lithuania and Latvia.

<u>Germany</u> – is a country in western central Europe. It is the second most populous country in Europe and has the largest economy of the continent.

<u>Poland</u> - is a country in central Europe.

<u>Latvia</u> – is a country in eastern Europe bordering the Baltic Sea.

<u>Russia</u> – is the largest country in the world. It encompasses Eastern Europe and Asia, thus a Eurasian country.

<u>Lithuania</u> – is a country in northern Europe. It is one of three Baltic states.

<u>Ukraine</u> – is located in Eastern Europe and borders the Black Sea.

<u>Honduras</u> – is a Central American country that borders Nicaragua to the north.

<u>Costa Rico</u> – is a country in Central America that borders Nicaragua to the south.

<u>Gulf of Mexico</u> – is the body of water that borders the United States, Mexico, and the island of Cuba.

<u>Caribbean</u> – is a suboceanic basin of the western Atlantic Ocean that borders Central and South America.

<u>Managua</u> – is the capital city of Nicaragua.

<u>Puerto Cabeza</u> – is an Atlantic coast city in northern Nicaragua.

<u>Cuba</u> – is an island nation located 90 miles from the state of Florida.

<u>Central America</u> – is an isthmus that connects North and South America.

<u>Lively Grove, Illinois</u> – is a small farming community located in southern Illinois about 40 miles from St. Louis Missouri.

<u>North Dakota</u> – is the 39th state admitted into the union of the United States. It is located in the northern United States and borders Canada.

<u>Dayton</u> – is a city in southwest Ohio located on the Great Miami River.

<u>Puerto Rico</u> – is a territory of the United States located in the northeaster Caribbean.

<u>Teguche/ Tegucigalpa</u> – is the capital city of Honduras.

<u>El Guasaule</u> – is a city in Nicaragua on the border with Honduras.

<u>San Sabastion de Yali</u> - a small city in north western Nicaragua.

El Salvador – is the smallest and most densely populated country in Central America.

Puerto Cortes – is a city on the Atlantic coast of Honduras.

Mexico City – is the capital city of Mexico.

Matamoras – is a city in northeastern Mexico.

San Antonio – is a city in south central Texas. It is the second most populous city in the state.

Texas – is the second largest state in the United States. It was admitted to the union of the United States in 1845.

Amarillo – is a city located in the panhandle of north Texas.

San Marcos – is a city in Texas between San Antonio and Austin.

Reynosa – is a border city in northern Mexico.

Brooks County – is located in south Texas near the border with Mexico.

Nederland – is a small community located in southeastern Texas.

McAllen – is a city located at the southern tip of Texas that borders Mexico.

Bexar County – is a county in Texas that encompasses the city of San Antonio.

Harlingen – is a city in southwestern Texas.

Martindale – is a small community in Texas east of San Marcos.

Things

Queue – is a braid of hair hanging down the back

Empress of China – is the name given to three ocean liners built for Canadian Pacific Steamships.

Hong Kong and Shanghai Banking Corporation Limited – was established in 1865 to fund the growing trade between China and Europe.

Bank of America (San Francisco) – was established in San Francisco in 1904 as the Bank of Italy. In 1928 it merged with Bank of America in Los Angeles.

USS Enterprise – was the sixth aircraft carrier to join the U.S. Navy fleet. It was commissioned in1936, but the author took poetic license to include it in the novel.

Nevada – was a U.S. Navy battleship launched in 1916. The ship served in World War I and World War II.

Arethusa – was a British battleship that saw action in World War II. Poet license was taken to include it in the ships seen at Pearl Harbor.

Star Bulletin – was the local Hawaii newspaper headquartered in Honolulu.

Scopes trial – was the 1925 trial regarding the right to teach evolution in the public schools in Tennessee. The lawyer for the defense was Clarence Darrow and the lawyer for the prosecution was William Jennings Bryan.

British lion – was a nickname given to Great Britain. The lion is a traditional symbol of Great Britain.

Spanish – referring to the official language of the country of Spain.

Chinese – referring to the official language of the country of China.

German – referring to official language of the country of Germany.

<u>English</u> – referring to the official language of the country of Great Britain.

<u>German U-boats</u> – were submarines used by the Germans in World War I and World War II.

<u>Missouri</u> – was the last battleship commissioned by the United States Navy. It was site of the surrender of Japan that ended World War II.

<u>Carter Administration</u> – refers to the U.S. presidency of Jimmy Carter from 1977-1981.

<u>Reagan Administration</u> – refers to the U.S. presidency of Ronald Reagan from

<u>C130</u> – is a military transport aircraft.

<u>Viet Nam war</u> – was a military conflict between North and South Vietnam from 1959-1973. The United States fought on the side of the South Vietnamese.

<u>SNAFU</u> – is an acronym meaning situation normal, all fouled (fucked) up.

<u>CO</u> – is a military acronym meaning commanding officer.

<u>MRE</u> – is an acronym for meal ready to eat; an individual field ration.

<u>Spam</u> – is a pre-cooked meat product, packaged in cans; it is made by Hormel Foods.

<u>M16</u> – is a United States military full- and semi-automatic rifle.

<u>M60</u> – is a United States military machine gun.

<u>Claymore mines</u> – are anti-personnel mines fired by remote control.

<u>M79</u> – is a single shot, shoulder fired grenade launcher.

<u>Ka-Bar</u> – is a combat knife first adopted by the U.S. Marines in 1942.

Starlight scope – is a night vision device.

Cordillera Isabella Mountains – a mountain range in central Nicaragua.

Desmoche – is a rummy card game that originated in Nicaragua and is often played for small stakes.

Universidad Nacional Autonoma de Nicaragua – is located in Managua. It is the main state-funded public university of Nicaragua.

El Chipote prison – is still an operational prison in Nicaragua.

Rio Coco – is the river boundary between Nicaragua and Honduras.

Rio Grande – is the river boundary between the United States/Texas border and Mexico.

Gulf of Honduras – is an inlet of the Caribbean Sea that borders Honduras, Belize, and Guatemala.

Toncontín International Airport – is a military and civilian airport that serves patrons of Tegucigalpa, Honduras.

Aeromexico – is the flag airline of Mexico based in Mexico City.

Eastern Airlines – was one of the big four airlines based in the United States that operated worldwide from 1930-1991.

Wells Fargo Bank – is a banking conglomerate that operates worldwide. It was founded in California in 1852.

NFL – is an acronym for the National Football League.

Political asylum – grants a person who is persecuted in his own country to be protected by and allowed entry into another country that has agreed to the United Nations Conventions Relating to the Status of Refugees.

<u>Javalinas</u> – or peccaries, are wild pig-like mammals prevalent in the southwestern United States, including Texas. They are social animals that form packs and can be extremely destructive and dangerous.

<u>DQ</u> – is an acronym for Dairy Queen, a fast food restaurant that specializes in soft-serve ice cream treats.

<u>Highway 80</u> – is a Texas highway that runs east and west from Karnes City to San Marcos.

<u>FM 1979</u> – is a farm to market Texas road located primarily in Guadalupe County in central Texas.

<u>Dallas Cowboy</u> – is a NFL football team based in Dallas, Texas.

<u>State Highway 1604</u> – is a state highway that circles the city of San Antonio.

<u>San Marcos River</u> – is a river in Central Texas that begins at springs in San Marcos and flows through Martindale enroute to where it merges with the Guadalupe River.

Resources

http://baseballhall.org/hof/mantle-mickey
http://christianity.about.com/od/biblestorysummaries/p/davidandgoliath.htm
http://cruiselinehistory.com/sailing-the-pacific-on-the-nyk-and-osk-lines-in-the-1920s-1930s/
http://cybersarges.tripod.com/25history.html
http://www.dallascowboys.com/
http://dictionary.reference.com/browse/queue
http://easternairlines.aero/
http://en.wikipedia.org/wiki/Aerom%C3%A9xico
http://en.wikipedia.org/wiki/Bai_Chongxi
http://en.wikipedia.org/wiki/Bank_of_America
http://en.wikipedia.org/wiki/British_Lions
http://en.wikipedia.org/wiki/Brooks_County,_Texas
http://en.wikipedia.org/wiki/China
http://en.wikipedia.org/wiki/Chinandega
http://en.wikipedia.org/wiki/CO
http://en.wikipedia.org/wiki/Costa_Rica
http://en.wikipedia.org/wiki/Dayton,_Ohio
http://en.wikipedia.org/wiki/Del_Norte_International_Airport
http://en.wikipedia.org/wiki/Desmoche
http://en.wikipedia.org/wiki/Education_in_Nicaragua
http://en.wikipedia.org/wiki/El_Salvador
http://en.wikipedia.org/wiki/Federales
http://en.wikipedia.org/wiki/Guangzhou
http://en.wikipedia.org/wiki/Honduras
http://en.wikipedia.org/wiki/Hong_Kong
http://en.wikipedia.org/wiki/Honolulu_Star-Bulletin

http://en.wikipedia.org/wiki/Ka-Bar
http://en.wikipedia.org/wiki/List_of_Farm_to_Market_Roads_in_Central_Texas
http://en.wikipedia.org/wiki/Lithuania
http://en.wikipedia.org/wiki/Lively_Grove,_Illinois
http://en.wikipedia.org/wiki/Longquan
http://en.wikipedia.org/wiki/M16_rifle
http://en.wikipedia.org/wiki/M18_Claymore_mine
http://en.wikipedia.org/wiki/M60_machine_gun
http://en.wikipedia.org/wiki/M79_grenade_launcher
http://en.wikipedia.org/wiki/Managua
http://en.wikipedia.org/wiki/Meal,_Ready-to-Eat
http://en.wikipedia.org/wiki/Mexico_City
http://en.wikipedia.org/wiki/Matamoros,_Tamaulipas
http://en.wikipedia.org/wiki/Mongol_invasions_and_co
nquests
http://en.wikipedia.org/wiki/Monterrey
http://en.wikipedia.org/wiki/National_Revolutionary_A
rmy
http://en.wikipedia.org/wiki/Night_vision_device
http://en.wikipedia.org/wiki/North_Dakota
http://en.wikipedia.org/wiki/Pearl_Harbor
http://en.wikipedia.org/wiki/Peccary
http://en.wikipedia.org/wiki/Puerto_Cabezas
http://en.wikipedia.org/wiki/Rail_transport_in_Central
_America
http://en.wikipedia.org/wiki/Rio_Grande
http://en.wikipedia.org/wiki/RMS_Empress_of_China_
%281890%29
http://en.wikipedia.org/wiki/Sanctuary_movement

http://en.wikipedia.org/wiki/Sandinista_National_Liber
ation_Front
http://en.wikipedia.org/wiki/San_Francisco
http://en.wikipedia.org/wiki/San_Marcos_River
http://en.wikipedia.org/wiki/San_Sebasti%C3%A1n_de
_Yal%C3%AD
http://en.wikipedia.org/wiki/South_China_Sea
http://en.wikipedia.org/wiki/Spam_%28food%29
http://en.wikipedia.org/wiki/Tegucigalpa
http://en.wikipedia.org/wiki/Texas
http://en.wikipedia.org/wiki/Texas_State_Highway_Loo
p_1604
http://en.wikipedia.org/wiki/Toncont%C3%ADn_Inter
national_Airport
http://en.wikipedia.org/wiki/USS_Missouri_%28BB-
63%29
http://en.wikipedia.org/wiki/USS_Nevada_%28BB-
36%29
http://en.wikipedia.org/wiki/History_of_Wells_Fargo
http://fas.org/man/dod-101/sys/ac/c-130.htm
http://forum.worldofwarships.com/index.php?/topic/101
58-august-9th-focus-arethusa-class-cruisers/
http://gocentralamerica.about.com/od/gettingtherearou
nd/a/Central-America-Border-Crossings.htm
https://libcom.org/history/1970-1987-the-contra-war-in-
nicaragua
http://memoryinlatinamerica.blogspot.com/2013/10/nica
ragua-proposal-to-turn-chipote.html
http://nicaraguadispatch.com/2013/10/nicaraguas-
opposition-wants-to-turn-jail-into-torture-museum/
http://www.baberuth.com/biography/

http://www.bbc.co.uk/history/historic_figures/chiang_k
aishek.shtml

http://www.belarus.by/en/about-belarus/geography

http://www.biography.com/people/fidel-castro-9241487

http://www.biography.com/people/george-custer-
9264128

http://www.biography.com/people/karl-marx-9401219

http://www.britannica.com/EBchecked/topic/95846/Cari
bbean-Sea

http://www.britannica.com/EBchecked/topic/129104/co
mmunism

http://www.britannica.com/EBchecked/topic/56027/Fulg
encio-Batista

http://www.britannica.com/EBchecked/topic/361411/Ma
nchu

http://www.britannica.com/EBchecked/topic/522138/Sa
ndinista

http://www.britannica.com/EBchecked/topic/612159/U-
boat

http://www.cbp.gov/border-security/along-us-
borders/overview

https://www.cia.gov/library/publications/the-world-
factbook/geos/cu.html

https://www.cia.gov/library/publications/the-world-
factbook/geos/gm.html

https://www.cia.gov/library/publications/the-world-
factbook/geos/lg.html

https://www.cia.gov/library/publications/the-world-
factbook/geos/pl.html

https://www.cia.gov/library/publications/the-world-
factbook/geos/rs.html

https://www.cia.gov/library/publications/the-world-factbook/geos/up.html

http://www.dairyqueen.com/us-en/Company/About-Us/

http://www.davidkopel.com/Misc/Nicaragua.htm

http://www.enterprise.navy.mil/

https://www.google.com/?gws_rd=ssl#q=amarillo+texas

https://www.google.com/?gws_rd=ssl#q=bexas+county+texas

https://www.google.com/?gws_rd=ssl#q=harlingen+texas

https://www.google.com/?gws_rd=ssl#q=mcallen+texas

https://www.google.com/?gws_rd=ssl#q=martindale+texas

https://www.google.com/?gws_rd=ssl#q=nederland+texas

https://www.google.com/?gws_rd=ssl#q=Puerto+Cortes+

https://www.google.com/?gws_rd=ssl#q=puerto+rico

https://www.google.com/?gws_rd=ssl#q=reynosa

https://www.google.com/?gws_rd=ssl#q=san+antonio+texas

https://www.google.com/?gws_rd=ssl#q=san+marcos+texas

https://www.google.com/webhp?sourceid=chrome-instant&rlz=1C1AVNA_enUS591US591&ion=1&espv=2&ie=UTF-8#q=state+highway+80+texas

https://www.google.com/webhp?sourceid=chrome-instant&rlz=1C1AVNA_enUS591US591&ion=1&espv=2&ie=UTF-8#q=gulf+of+honduras

https://www.google.com/webhp?sourceid=chrome-instant&rlz=1C1AVNA_enUS591US591&ion=1&espv=2&ie=UTF-8#q=political+asylum

https://www.google.com/webhp?sourceid=chrome-instant&rlz=1C1AVNA_enUS591US591&ion=1&espv=2&ie=UTF-8#q=rio+coco

https://www.google.com/webhp?sourceid=chrome-instant&rlz=1C1AVNA_enUS591US591&ion=1&espv=2&ie=UTF-8#gs_ssp=eJzj4tDP1TewNDM0BgAJTgHh&q=three+stooges

http://www.gulfbase.org/facts.php

http://www.history.com/topics/maya

http://www.history.com/topics/world-war-ii/nazi-party

http://www.history.com/topics/vietnam-war

http://www.hsbc.com.hk/1/2/about/home/hsbc-s-history

http://www.imdb.com/name/nm0000078/bio

http://www.lonelyplanet.com/nicaragua/to-somotillo-el-guasaule-honduran-border

http://www.merriam-webster.com/dictionary/snafu

http://www.merriam-webster.com/dictionary/socialism

http://www.merriam-webster.com/dictionary/soviet

http://www.morgansrock.com/local-food-nicaragua/88-the-food-of-nicaragua-la-comida-nica.html

http://www.nationalreview.com/article/383655/coyotes-lure-illegal-immigrants-promises-amnesty-ryan-lovelace

http://www.nfl.com/

http://www.nicaragua.com/mountains/

http://www.nytimes.com/1988/09/25/books/underground-railroad-1980-s-style.html?pagewanted=2

http://www.pbs.org/wgbh/evolution/library/08/2/l_082_01.html

http://www.scrapbook.com/poems/doc/3061.html

http://www.urbandictionary.com/define.php?term=Wet back

https://www.whitehouse.gov/1600/presidents/herbertho over

https://www.whitehouse.gov/1600/presidents/jimmycart er

https://www.whitehouse.gov/1600/presidents/ronaldreag an

http://www.worldatlas.com/webimage/countrys/cameric a.htm